KIDNAPPED!

Elizabeth unfastened the chain lock as Carl became aware of what was happening.

"No!" he cried as he rose to prevent her escape. "Elizabeth, no!"

She unlocked the bolt and pulled on the door handle. It wouldn't be long before she was free.

But something was wrong. The door wouldn't open! Elizabeth gasped as Carl seized her. He grabbed her under the arms and threw her onto the sofa with the force of a man possessed. His eyes now bright with anger, he came toward her.

This is it, thought Elizabeth as she squeezed her eyes shut. *This is the end.*

Bantam Books in the Sweet Valley High Series
Ask your bookseller for the books you have missed

#1 DOUBLE LOVE
#2 SECRETS
#3 PLAYING WITH FIRE
#4 POWER PLAY
#5 ALL NIGHT LONG
#6 DANGEROUS LOVE
#7 DEAR SISTER
#8 HEARTBREAKER
#9 RACING HEARTS
#10 WRONG KIND OF GIRL
#11 TOO GOOD TO BE TRUE
#12 WHEN LOVE DIES
#13 KIDNAPPED!
#14 DECEPTIONS
#15 PROMISES
#16 RAGS TO RICHES
#17 LOVE LETTERS
#18 HEAD OVER HEELS
#19 SHOWDOWN
#20 CRASH LANDING!
#21 RUNAWAY
#22 TOO MUCH IN LOVE
#23 SAY GOODBYE
#24 MEMORIES
#25 NOWHERE TO RUN
#26 HOSTAGE!
#27 LOVESTRUCK
#28 ALONE IN THE CROWD
#29 BITTER RIVAL
#30 JEALOUS LIES
#31 TAKING SIDES

Super Edition: PERFECT SUMMER
Super Edition: SPECIAL CHRISTMAS
Super Edition: SPRING BREAK
Super Edition: MALIBU SUMMER

SWEET VALLEY HIGH

KIDNAPPED!

Written by
Kate William

Created by
FRANCINE PASCAL

BANTAM BOOKS
TORONTO · NEW YORK · LONDON · SYDNEY · AUCKLAND

RL7, IL age 12 and up

KIDNAPPED
A Bantam Book / April 1984

Sweet Valley High is a trademark of Francine Pascal

Conceived by Francine Pascal

Produced by Cloverdale Press, Inc.

Cover art by James Mathewuse

ISBN 0-553-26619-5

Published simultaneously in the United States and Canada

Bantam Books are published by Bantam Books, Inc. Its trademark, consisting of
the words "Bantam Books" and the portrayal of a rooster, is Registered in
U.S. Patent and Trademark Office and in other countries. Marca Registrada.
Bantam Books, Inc., 666 Fifth Avenue, New York, New York 10103.

PRINTED IN THE UNITED STATES OF AMERICA

O   17 16 15 14 13 12 11 10 9 8

To Matthew Young

One

"Steve, can you help me with this zipper, please?" Jessica Wakefield called as she raced down the hall to her brother's room. With one hand holding up the top of her blue silk dress, she rushed into Steven's bedroom. "It seems to be stuck—" Jessica paused as she looked around and saw no trace of her brother. "Steven? Don't tell me you've left already!" She fell on his bed, tossing aside his plaid comforter in annoyance.

"Hey, relax, Jess. I'm in here." Steven pushed open the door to his tiny bathroom. His hair still wet from his shower, a green towel wrapped snugly around his waist, Steven stopped shaving for a moment as he spoke to his sister. "Give me another minute. Then I'll rescue you

1

from whatever crisis you've managed to get yourself into. What is it this time?"

Jessica caught his patronizing tone and didn't like it. "Very funny, Steve. I'll bet you think you're a real comedian."

Steven made one last stroke with his razor. "No, just your older brother," he said, wiping his face. "See, Jess, sometimes you have a tendency to treat a little thing like a national emergency. What's the big deal?"

The big deal, thought Jessica, *is only the most exciting, most important party of the year.* But Steven wouldn't understand. And Jessica didn't feel like arguing with him. The evening promised to be too good to get it started on the wrong foot. "Could you zip up my dress, please?" she asked again, making her voice as sweet as maple syrup.

"Your better half isn't around to do it?" Steven asked, referring to Elizabeth, Jessica's identical twin.

"I'll bet you never call me *Liz's* better half," Jessica responded sulkily. "But anyway, she's still at the hospital."

"I thought you guys just worked there on weekdays."

"We do, but Liz offered to go in today for some nurse's aide who went on vacation," Jessica said, rising from the bed. "Though why she did that when there was this big party

2

tonight, I'll never know. But that's our sister. Always the good Samaritan."

"Isn't that what working as a candy striper is all about? Good Samaritanism?"

"Oh, Steven." Jessica sighed. "There's much more to it than that." *Much more*, she thought to herself with delicious amusement.

Jessica had decided to volunteer at the hospital after learning that Jeremy Frank, a well-known and—not coincidentally—handsome Sweet Valley TV personality, was laid up there with a broken leg. She'd convinced her twin to become a candy striper too; and while Elizabeth was busy dedicating herself to her work, Jessica was busy dedicating herself to the pursuit of Jeremy Frank. In the end her plans for romance had backfired, but she'd wound up with something just as good—an offer to appear on Jeremy's TV talk show to discuss what it was like to be a teenager. She'd returned from taping the show earlier that afternoon and was still flying high.

Jessica turned her attention back to Steven. "No, there's a lot more to being a candy striper than being a good Samaritan. It's also hard work and very time-consuming." Then, sighing dramatically, she added, "I'm not sure how much longer I'll be able to do it. But I admire Liz for her dedication."

"Right." Steven rubbed a towel through his

3

dark hair. Sometimes he didn't believe half of what Jessica told him.

"So can you help me, please?" Jessica asked again.

"Sure," Steven said good-naturedly. He walked up to his sister, who was now standing before the full-length mirror on the back of his closet door. He bent his six-foot-one body over her zipper. It took a little maneuvering, but he finally managed to zip up the dress without damaging the delicate fabric. "You had a thread caught in it," he told her.

"Thank you, Steve," she said, admiring herself in the mirror. "What do you think?"

Steven inspected his sister carefully. Jessica had a knack for picking out clothes that made her look her best—although even a burlap sack couldn't conceal her perfectly proportioned figure. This dress was no exception. The iridescent material matched her brilliant, blue-green eyes, and the neckline of the sleeveless dress was about as low as a sixteen-year-old could get away with.

"Nice," was what Steven told her.

"Nice?" she echoed bitingly. "Is that *all* you can say?"

Steven laughed. "Oh, come on, Jess. You know you look great. Really, you do."

"That's more like it." Jessica grinned.

"But have Mom and Dad seen that dress?"

4

Steven continued. "It looks a little—um—grown-up to me."

"Oh, Steven, would you stop treating me as if I were a baby? What would you like me to wear, bib overalls?"

"Now, Jessica, I just meant that it looks a little, uh—"

"Sexy?" Jessica cut in. "Alluring, perhaps?"

"You're putting it mildly, Jess. The way you look, you'll be fighting off at least ninety percent of the guys in Sweet Valley."

"I'm not interested in ninety percent," Jessica said, flicking a stray strand of her golden blond hair off her forehead. "Just one."

"Anyone I know?"

"Nicholas Morrow."

"Morrow." Steven repeated the name softly. "Aren't they the family who just took over the old Godfrey estate?"

"That's right. Regina Morrow is giving a party tonight. She's my age and starting at Sweet Valley High next week. Nicholas is eighteen. I can't wait to meet him."

"You mean to tell me you're going to all this trouble for a perfect stranger?" Jessica nodded, and Steven continued. "That's a first, isn't it? I mean, what if this Nicholas guy turns out to be a real nerd?"

"He isn't, Steve. I checked around and have it on good authority that he's gorgeous. Furthermore, he's fabulously rich. What could be wrong with him?"

Steven shot Jessica a disgusted look and didn't bother to answer. He wished his sister would learn that money and good looks weren't the only things that made someone desirable. Steven knew better than most that even the poorest people could have riches that couldn't be calculated in dollars and cents. He conjured up a picture of his girlfriend, Tricia Martin. She was dirt poor, but she was the loveliest, kindest girl Steven had ever met. Still thinking about Tricia, Steven glanced at his clock. "Uh, Jess, I don't mean to kick you out of my room or anything, but I've got to get dressed. I promised Tricia I'd be at her place by seven-thirty."

Jessica fought to hold back the distaste she'd always felt for her brother's girlfriend. She had never understood how he could have fallen for someone from a family like Tricia's. Besides being practically penniless, the Martins had a bad reputation. Mr. Martin had become an alcoholic after his wife died, and Tricia's sister, Betsy, was in and out of trouble with the Sweet Valley police. Elizabeth insisted that Tricia was different from the rest of her family, but Jessica still couldn't bear to have her brother's name linked with the Martins'. In the past Jessica had never hesitated to express feelings. But things were different now, and she felt she owed her brother the courtesy of silence on the issue. They'd both just learned that Tricia was dying of leukemia, and nothing anyone could do or say could keep Steven from being with her as often as possible.

"How's she feeling?" Jessica asked.

"Tired," Steven answered. "We're probably just going to spend the evening at her place."

"Well, I hope you have a good time tonight. I know I will," Jessica said breezily. She glided out of Steven's room and headed toward her own.

Jessica breathed a sigh of relief as she closed the door behind her. She was glad Steven hadn't pressed her on the dress. It *was* very revealing, and she'd deliberately waited to dress until after her parents had left to go out to dinner. As soon as their car backed out of their driveway, she'd hurried to her room and slipped into the dress. She was sure they'd have forbidden her to wear it, but nothing was going to stop her from going all out that night. Jessica was determined to be the center of attention at this party.

Retreating to her bathroom, which she shared with Elizabeth, Jessica rummaged through the vanity drawer for a decent shade of nail polish. After carefully examining every bottle there, she finally chose a hot-rose shade. *I hope Nicholas likes it*, she said to herself as she spread the smooth lacquer on her fingernails.

Nicholas Morrow. Even the name sounded

gorgeous, she thought. She really knew next to nothing about him, except that he had grown up somewhere on the East Coast. Boston, her father had said.

Her father, Ned Wakefield, a prominent lawyer in town, had handled all the legal work involved in the sale of the house Nicholas now lived in—though "house" was the wrong word for it, Jessica reflected. "Castle" was more like it. She'd been in the house only once, when she'd tagged along with her father during a business call to its former owner, Morgan Godfrey. That was shortly before Godfrey died five years ago, and as far as she knew, no one had been inside it all this time.

The estate was the largest in Sweet Valley, even larger than the manors owned by the wealthiest families in town, the Patmans and the Fowlers. Godfrey had inherited part of a vast fortune, but had left no heirs of his own. No family in the area had had enough money to take over the estate—until now.

The grounds were near the Patman estate, and when Jessica had been dating Bruce Patman—in a tumultuous and short-lived relationship—she'd seen part of the old mansion from the top of the Patmans' hill. It was still majestic looking, even though the fountains in the front had been turned off and most of the mansion walls were covered with wild ivy that had been untrimmed for years. But all it needed was a little tender loving care to turn it into a show-place again.

Jessica's daydreams were interrupted by a knock on her door. "Jess, I'm leaving now," she heard Steven call. She stepped into her bedroom and caught her brother leaning half-way into her room. "How do I look?" he asked.

"Nice," she said, parroting his earlier remark, though she really thought her brother was the most handsome guy in Sweet Valley. Steven was dressed casually in a pair of jeans and a plaid shirt. His black-leather aviator jacket was flung over his shoulder.

"I should have known better than to ask you," he said, grinning. "Well, I've got to run, or I'll be late."

Jessica slipped into a pair of open-toed, navy heels. "What time is it, anyhow, Steven?"

"Since when are you interested in the time?"

"Since right now. I don't want to be late for the party."

"Want a lift over there?"

"No. I promised Liz I'd wait for her. I just hope she gets here soon."

Steven raised an eyebrow. "Haven't I heard you say that a party never really starts until you get there? No matter when that is?" He shook his head. "This Morrow guy must really be important to you." Steven checked his wristwatch. "Well, for what it's worth, it's exactly seven-fourteen. When's Liz due home?"

"Is that all!" Jessica threw her arms up in near-anguish. "Liz won't be back till eight. She said she'd be finishing up at the hospital around six, and then she had to stop at Max Dellon's house to help him study for an English test."

"Another act of good Samaritanism?" Steven asked.

"Well, Mr. Collins practically begged her to tutor Max. I guess I can understand her not being able to say no to that man," Jessica said, picturing the handsome teacher whom she'd always considered Sweet Valley's contribution toward beautifying America, "though why I agreed to wait for her, I'll never know."

"You sure you don't want a ride?"

"No, I'd better wait."

Steven shrugged. "You can't say I didn't offer. Have a good time."

Jessica smiled. "You too, Steve." She squeezed his arm to let him know she shared his pain.

"Don't forget to put a coat over that dress," he said, forcing a smile. "It's cold outside."

"OK, big brother," she said. Actually for a while Jessica had contemplated making a grand entrance wearing only the dress, thinking wickedly about how the sight of her cold, shivering body would prompt Nicholas to rush up and put his arms around her to warm her up. But evenings at this time of year were usually chilly, and she saw no reason to risk pneumonia just for a sympathy hug. She'd have to settle for throwing her coat off dramatically as she was being ushered into the Morrow mansion. In any event, she was confident that by the time the night was over she'd come up with at least a dozen other good ways to lure Nicholas into her arms. And if her dress didn't do the trick, her new black-and-white bikini would. She knew from her father that the Morrows had a fabulous indoor pool, and Regina's invitation had said to bring a bathing suit. Jessica had selected her most alluring one just for the occasion.

After she put on her makeup, Jessica pranced down the stairs to the kitchen. The clock read seven-thirty. She stood looking at the clock and clicking her fingernails restlessly on the kitchen counter. She wished her sister would hurry up and get home. Suddenly, as she thought about Elizabeth, a strange cold, little shiver went through Jessica's body. She tried to shrug it off, but the nagging feeling wouldn't go away. This happened to her once in a while, and it usually meant that something was troubling her twin. Jessica and Elizabeth saw themselves as flip sides of the same coin, and they picked up on each other's moods in an almost uncanny way.

Jessica decided to call Elizabeth at Max's to find out what was going on. She went to the wall phone, picked it up, and began to dial but then put the receiver down. As Steven had indicated earlier, she did tend to overreact. It was probably nothing serious. In all likelihood, the tutoring session was going less smoothly than Elizabeth would have liked. As she thought about it more, Jessica concluded that butting in with a phone call would only make matters worse. Elizabeth and Max might be disturbed by the interruption and have to start over from scratch. That meant Elizabeth would come home even later than she'd planned. And time was paramount.

Well, at least, Jessica figured, she could speed things up. She flew upstairs to Elizabeth's bedroom and began riffling through her sister's neatly organized closet. *Now Elizabeth won't have to waste time choosing an outfit*, Jessica told herself, as she fingered a long, red velour skirt. It wasn't the type of thing Jessica would have picked for herself, but she felt her more traditional sister would love it. A few hangers down the rack, Jessica found an off-white, high-necked blouse that completed the outfit.

Jessica lay the clothes on Elizabeth's bed and admired her selection. *She'll look fantastic tonight*, Jessica assured herself, though she couldn't help thinking that it wasn't the traffic-stopping outfit she had decided on for herself.

What was more important to Jessica, however,

was that she would save her twin at least ten minutes of rummaging through her closet. They'd get to the party that much earlier. As an afterthought, Jessica laid her sister's turquoise tank suit on top of the rest of the outfit. Now everything was ready.

At a quarter to eight, Jessica headed downstairs to wait for her sister in the living room. Through the Haitian white curtains she saw the bright beam of headlights as a car rounded the corner and headed down her street. She breathed a sigh of relief. *Good old Elizabeth. As reliable as the sun, and home at last.*

But it wasn't Elizabeth. The car neared and then passed the Wakefield house without stopping.

Jessica flicked on the television set to divert her mind. But after a minute or two, she switched off the set impatiently and threw the remote-control wand onto the sofa.

At ten minutes to eight Jessica could stand it no longer. The house was giving her a monumental case of claustrophobia. She had to get to the party and couldn't wait for her twin. A promise was a promise, but she had so convinced herself that Max Dellon's ignorance would tie up her twin for the next several hours that she felt she had the right to leave immediately.

Jessica ran to the phone, dialed, and was glad when her best friend, Cara Walker, picked

13

it up on the first ring. "Hi, Cara," she said. "You ready for the party?"

"All dressed up and just about to leave."

"Great. I've got a favor to ask. Would you mind picking me up? Liz just called and told me she's going to be late." Jessica crossed her fingers as she spoke.

"Sure. I'll be right over."

"Great!"

As soon as Jessica got off the phone with Cara, she hurried back to the kitchen. She ripped a piece of paper from the message pad next to the wall phone and scribbled out a note for her sister.

"Dear Liz," she wrote. "Something came up. Got a ride with Cara. See you at the party. Love, J."

Jessica folded the note and left it on the kitchen table, where Elizabeth was sure to see it when she got home.

Two

Cara pulled up in front of Jessica's house a few minutes later. She beeped her horn twice and was amazed to see Jessica instantly appear at the door.

Her white wool coat wrapped around her and her canvas carryall flung over her shoulder, Jessica flew down the path and ran toward Cara's car. Her cheeks were flushed by the unusually chilly air.

"Is your house on fire? The only other place I've seen you run out of so quickly is Mr. Russo's chemistry class."

"I couldn't wait any longer. I'm ready to party."

"Ready to meet Nicholas Morrow, you mean." Cara winked playfully as she put the car in gear and headed toward the Morrow estate.

Cara was well aware of Jessica's interest in the new boy in town. How could she not be? She'd accompanied Jessica to her television taping that afternoon, and during the breaks, Nicholas was all Jessica could talk about. Cara was glad he had taken her friend's mind off Jeremy Frank. She felt the TV personality was too old for Jessica and that he'd never see her as anything more than a cute kid.

Jessica hadn't minded pouring her heart out to Cara, either. She knew her friend would keep her hands off Nicholas. The two girls had an unwritten rule that served them well: Thou Shalt Not Chase After the Same Boy as Your Best Friend. So far it had worked, much to Jessica's relief. Although she considered herself the more desirable of the two, Jessica realized that Cara could be formidable opposition. With her thick mane of dark, glossy hair and eye-catching figure, she was used to turning a few heads herself.

"There ought to be plenty of other guys left for you," Jessica told Cara as they turned up the road that led to the hill where the town's elite lived, a magnificent expanse of land high above the rest of Sweet Valley. "Everybody'll be there."

"I'm ready," Cara said with a trace of wistfulness. "Maybe this time I'll find someone who wants me."

"Feeling sorry for yourself is not allowed in this car," Jessica said. Ordinarily she might have flung one of her sarcastic barbs at Cara, but she held back. Recently Jessica had practically forced Steven to go out with her friend, and it had been a disaster. Jessica knew Cara was still upset. "Look, it's not my fault my stupid brother can't see how good you'd be for him. Maybe after Tricia dies, you two could start over again."

"Jessica, that's morbid!"

"No, that's life, Cara," Jessica said matter-of-factly. "We all know she's going to die, and afterward my poor brother is going to need someone to help him pick up the pieces. It might as well be you."

"Forget it, Jess. No one's going to call me a grave robber." Cara made a sharp right-hand turn onto a long road that gradually wound upward. Suddenly the girls were in full view of the sparkling lights of the houses below them. "Wow, it's beautiful up here."

Jessica looked out the window at the view she never tired of. "The house should be coming up in about a mile. The driveway is the first one past Bruce's house."

"I know," Cara said as she tapped her foot lightly on the brake.

"Hey, hurry up, would you?"

Cara had slowed down to about twenty miles an hour. The road was dark and full of curves, with massive Douglas firs standing like sentries along its edge, guarding the privacy of the houses nestled behind them. Cara was taking no chances.

"Look, if you're worried about someone beating us to the Morrows, I think you can relax. As you can see, we're the only ones on the road right now." Cara drove slowly past the stone-columned iron gate of the Patman estate. "We'll meet Nicholas and Regina soon enough."

"I wonder what kind of girl Regina Morrow is," Jessica said. "I hope she's fun."

"I don't think she'd be throwing this party if she were a hermit."

"I know that. I meant that it would be helpful if I get off to a good start with her. It'll make things easier when I go out with Nicholas. Maybe we can even double-date."

"Whoa, Jess. Aren't you jumping the gun a little? He hasn't asked you out yet."

Jessica flashed one of her know-it-all smiles. "But he will."

Cara didn't bother to respond. She knew Jessica was like the Royal Canadian Mounted Police —she always got her man.

A few minutes later Cara made a left turn onto the road that led to the Morrow estate. After passing through a large open iron gate similar to the Patmans', she drove another half mile down a narrow, winding, blacktopped driveway lined on both sides with tall hedges. The

18

bushes blocked the view of the house until Cara made a final turn. Then the hedges gave way to a garden-lined, circular driveway. Before them stood a modern Xanadu.

Cara slowed the car for a moment as the girls took in the sight. Several large, ground-based floodlights bathed the three-story structure with an amber glow. The honey-colored stone mansion was enormous, with two giant wings extending from a central structure fronted by three massive marble columns. Gone were the weeds that had threatened to overwhelm what was now a seemingly endless expanse of emerald-green lawn. Flanking the main entrance were twin rows of neatly manicured cypress trees, all planted in huge brass urns. In the center of the circular drive were three pure-white marble fountains that sprayed mists of water into the crisp night air.

Cara was awestruck. "Have you ever seen anything like it, Jess?"

The usually nonchalant Jessica was equally impressed. "God, what I would do to live in a place like this."

"And get a load of that!" As she drove closer, Cara pointed to the five-car garage at the far end of the house. Parked outside in the driveway was a sleek red Ferrari 308/GT that stood out like a fireball against the night sky.

"Nice," agreed Jessica. *So Nicholas lives in the*

fast lane, she thought. His appeal was growing with each passing second. "I'd love to see him go one-on-one with Bruce and his Porsche."

"I'll bet you would." Cara giggled.

The conversation was cut short by a uniformed man who opened Cara's door. "Hmm, valet service," Cara said, giving Jessica an OK sign with her fingers. The night promised to be first class all the way.

Jessica couldn't wait to get inside. She strode quickly up the wide stone steps that led to the front door. She was about to ring the bell when the intricately cut mahogany door opened.

A strikingly good-looking couple, about the age of her parents, Jessica guessed, stepped toward the two girls. "Oh, excuse me," Mr. Morrow said. "I didn't know anyone was here. We were just on our way out."

Jessica was transfixed momentarily by the magnetism of the man's bright-blue eyes. They were the dominant feature of his tanned, youthful-looking face, a face that had success written all over it. Snapping back to attention, Jessica said, "We don't want to keep you."

"Not to worry," the man said, smiling. "I'm always glad to meet Regina's friends. You're the first to arrive."

Jessica breathed a deep sigh of relief.

"By the way, I'm Regina's father, Kurt Morrow. And this is my wife, Skye." The tall, dark-eyed woman stood silent at his side, her body wrapped cocoonlike in a full-length, black sable coat.

"I know, Mr. Morrow," Jessica said, wondering if the expression "like father like son" had any relevance in the Morrow household. She recalled her father mentioning that Kurt Morrow had once been a professional football player, and time had done little to diminish his attractive athletic build. "You're exactly like my father described you. I'm Jessica Wakefield, and this is my friend Cara Walker."

"So you're Jessica." Mr. Morrow nodded approvingly. "Your father has told me all about you and your sister. Sorry I can't stay to chat, but we're already late for our party. Please go right in and make yourselves at home."

"Regina and Nicholas are still upstairs, but they should be down any minute," Mrs. Morrow added with a tight smile as she and her husband moved down the front steps.

Jessica and Cara found themselves standing alone in a central hall whose highly polished marble floor reflected the bright lights of the intricately cut crystal chandelier overhead. "God, Jess, you could fit my entire house in this room," Cara said, gasping.

"May I take your coats, girls?"

Jessica whipped around and found herself face-to-face with a small, elderly man in a butler's uniform. "The party is this way," he announced in a clipped, vaguely British accent. "Come along with me."

The man looked as if he could hardly stand, yet he guided the girls past the dining room, the library, the billiards room, and a room he referred to as the sitting parlor before they got to the den. "I've been here a week, and I still get confused," the man said with a little laugh.

The usual names for the rooms seemed highly inappropriate. The den was, in size and feeling, more like the main room in an exclusive private club. On one wall was a rough-stone fireplace, the blazing logs casting a warm glow in the room. Antique Oriental rugs covered the dark wood floor, and on the walnut-paneled walls were several Renaissance paintings. Yet the room was anything but forbidding. Several overstuffed velvet couches and chairs lined two walls; the remaining wall housed a stereo, a TV, a bar, and a bank of four arcade-style video games. A glass doorway at one end of the den led to an indoor swimming pool under a crystal-clear skylight.

"Not too shabby," Cara said, reaching for one of the miniature pastries arranged on a silver tray at one end of the bar. Next to the pastries was another tray, filled with chips and raw vegetables, and a bowl of dip.

"Nope. Not bad at all," agreed Jessica as they were joined in the den by a beautiful girl of about their own age. She had long, wavy, black hair, a porcelain complexion, and dancing blue eyes. Her black silk jumpsuit fit her tall, statuesque body perfectly.

Smiling graciously, she greeted her guests, focusing first on Cara. "Please excuse me. I'm Regina, and you're—?"

"Cara. Cara Walker," she finished. "Uh, nice place you've got here."

Regina giggled. "Isn't it?"

"You're so lucky," Cara continued. "Is your room anything like this?"

Regina's large eyes grew even wider. "Oh, no," she said. "I don't have a stereo."

"Do you have a view?" Cara asked.

"Yes. Of the valley. It's beautiful," Regina said, directing all her attention to Cara. The sparkle in her eyes reflected that she didn't take her luxurious surroundings for granted.

Jessica was puzzled. Regina was so friendly with Cara but seemed to be ignoring her. She could see she'd have to step in and introduce herself. "I can't wait to see it," she said, speaking at Regina's side. "By the way, I'm Jessica Wakefield."

Regina acted as though she hadn't heard her. "Do you live near here?" she asked Cara.

"Down there." Cara pointed out the window in the general direction of the bottom of the hill.

"So do I," Jessica said, uncomfortable about having to follow Cara's lead.

Regina moved away from the window to reach for a pastry. As she walked, her heel caught the edge of one of the carpets, causing her to stumble. She recovered quickly, though.

"By the way, where's your brother?" Jessica asked.

Regina didn't answer, and that made Jessica fume. *What's wrong with this girl?* she wondered. *Why is she treating me like dirty dishwater?* Then she began to piece it together. The stumble, the lack of response to Jessica— It was only natural to conclude that the Morrow girl was drunk.

"Say, Regina," Jessica called. She took a few steps toward her and tapped her on the shoulder. "Where are you hiding the booze?"

Regina looked dumbfounded. "Sorry," she said seriously, "it's not that kind of party. My parents would kill me. May I get you a soda?" She walked to the refrigerator behind the bar and opened the door. A moment later she stood up. "I'm sorry. Did you tell me what kind you wanted?"

Jessica looked at her strangely. "I didn't say a word."

Regina leaned over the bar and smiled sheepishly. "I wasn't sure, since I had my back turned to you. You see, I'm deaf."

The two other girls were stunned. "But you can understand us!" Cara finally said.

"Yes," Regina answered, handing Cara a cold soft drink. "I read lips. And I can hear certain sounds, but they don't make any sense to me. It's been described to me as something like a radio that's not quite tuned in."

"You poor thing," Jessica said, with utmost sincerity. "How awful for you."

"It's not so bad," Regina said. "I mean, you can't miss what you never had. I've been deaf since birth. And it does have its advantages. I don't have to put up with boring lectures or TV commercials. But there's a disadvantage, too. I never stopped to think about getting a band to play for this party. I hope you're not disappointed."

"It's just as well," Cara said. "The only decent band in the area is a group called The Droids, and they're temporarily out of commission." Answering Regina's look of confusion, she added, "Their guitarist, Max Dellon, has been grounded until he gets his grades up."

"We'll have to make do with my brother's records." Regina pointed to the case next to the turntable, which contained enough albums to supply a radio station for a month.

Regina seemed so good-natured about her handicap that Jessica could hardly believe it.

25

Then a horrible thought entered her mind. "Is Nicholas deaf, too?" she asked.

"No, I'm not."

Jessica turned around and got her first look at Adonis personified. Like Regina, he was blessed with a full head of black, wavy hair, which he wore swept back off his face, the waves falling in perfect layers down to the nape of his neck. From his piercing, deep-set, emerald-green eyes to the cleft in his chin he had a face that would make any male model burn with envy.

He went straight to Jessica and shook her hand. "I see you've already met my sister. I'm Nicholas Morrow."

"Jessica Wakefield." She shot a quick glance at Cara, who, reading the signal correctly, cornered Regina at the bar and continued their conversation.

Turning back to Nicholas, Jessica said, sincerely, "I hope you weren't offended by what I said. It's just that I've never met a deaf person before, and it sort of slipped out."

"Believe me, I've heard worse," Nicholas said. "I'm glad you're honest about your feelings. Lots of people shy away from Regina because of her deafness."

"She seems able to handle it fine, but I can't help thinking it's got to be tough for her."

"My sister is a trouper," Nicholas said with obvious pride in his voice. "It was really rough when she was little. You know, kids making fun of her and all. She had to be tough to survive, and she did it, learning how to read lips and get along in what the deaf call 'the speaking world.' She went to a special school until she reached junior high and then begged our parents to let her go to regular school. Mom was really against it, but Regina stuck to her guns and won out."

Jessica studied Nicholas as he talked. It was not just his physical features that made him so appealing; Nicholas's primary attractiveness came from within. He had an aura of intelligence that showed in the self-assured way he carried himself and spoke. There was no trace of the artificial exuberance of someone out to prove how rich and handsome he was.

Nicholas glanced at Regina, who was watching Cara's lips attentively. "My sister did really well in Boston," he said. "I hope things work out as nicely for her here."

"You really care about her, don't you?"

Nicholas looked down at Jessica and nodded. "She's a very special girl."

"Then first thing Monday morning I'll take her around and introduce her to all the PBA girls."

"What's that?"

"Pi Beta Alpha. It's the best sorority at Sweet Valley High. I'm the president, and with a little

27

bit of string pulling, I think I can get Regina admitted." She looked up at Nicholas for approval, but his face was taut.

"Regina doesn't need your pity, Jessica." He began to move away.

"I don't pity her," Jessica said, defending herself. Nicholas stopped to listen. "In fact, I'm a little envious. A girl that pretty could be tough competition." She wasn't going to admit that her prime motivation for helping Regina was to please Nicholas. But Jessica was also impressed with his sister's spunk, and she had a feeling she might like Regina anyway. "You can ask anyone around here. I'm very selective when it comes to PBA pledges."

Nicholas threw up his hands. "I plead guilty to big-brotheritis. I guess I was overreacting. It's just that it's happened so many times before." He put a hand on Jessica's shoulder. "I apologize."

"No need to," Jessica said, smiling. "I have an older brother, too. In fact, he's the same age as you."

"How do you know how old I am?" Nicholas asked curiously.

"Oh, I believe my father told me," Jessica explained. "He did all the paperwork on this house for your dad."

"That's right. I thought the name Wakefield sounded familiar. Do you have any sisters?"

"My sister, Elizabeth. We're identical twins."

"Really?" Nicholas's eyes grew wide. "I'd love to meet her."

"Oh, she'll be here anytime now," Jessica said, feeling a tiny twinge of guilt at not having waited for her. But Elizabeth would understand. She always did.

Three

Elizabeth Wakefield tried desperately to remember what had happened to her. But she couldn't recall anything that took place after she'd gotten into her car. Through the stifling fog that filled her brain, she forced herself to try to think clearly, but her head was spinning and her body was numb. All she knew was that dressed in her pink-and-white candy striper's uniform, she had headed out the double-doored side entrance of Fowler Memorial Hospital. She had been greeted with a cold blast of wind and wished she hadn't left her sweater in the car. But it had been an understandable omission. When she'd entered the hospital that afternoon, the day had been bright, warm, and sunny, and she'd decided she wouldn't need the sweater.

But by the time she left, there were thunder-clouds overhead.

But she hadn't been totally unprepared. She'd had a cream-colored scarf stashed in her pocket-book, which she tied hastily around her neck. Then, with her arms clutched close to her body, she had walked briskly across the parking lot to her red Fiat Spider.

The lot was nearly deserted, and the only other vehicle in sight was an old, beat-up, gun-metal-gray van parked next to her car. She was in a hurry and just glanced briefly at it. She had to stop at Max Dellon's house for a tutoring session before heading home to get ready for the party she would attend that evening. She was running late.

Jessica is going to kill me, she thought as she put her key in the door lock. She'd promised her twin a ride to the party, and she knew Jessica wanted to get there as soon as possible.

She'd thought briefly about calling Jessica and telling her to find another way to the party, but she changed her mind at the last minute. It was a long walk back to the hospital. She was cold. And she had no time to waste.

Once inside the car, Elizabeth blew on her hands to warm them before starting up the motor. She put her key in the ignition. And— The images faded. Elizabeth's memory went blank. She tried to open her eyes, but something was preventing her from seeing. She shook her head frantically as if to push away the dark cloud that seemed to envelop her. But still she couldn't focus on anything. She tried to raise a hand to her eyes, but she couldn't. It was then that the nightmarish realization hit her. Her arms were tied behind her back, and she was blindfolded. She took several deep breaths to stave off the panic that threatened to engulf her. Her head cleared a little. She willed herself to stay levelheaded and take stock of the situation.

Where am I? she thought, fighting a consuming feeling of terror. The air was dank and cool but not as bitingly cold as it had been outdoors. It smelled of musty cigarette smoke mixed with a pungent odor she didn't recognize. The surface underneath her was rocking. It felt as if she were moving—in some sort of vehicle.

Suddenly the memory rushed back—the dark silhouette of a large man. She had tried to scream, but before she could, he had clamped something over her mouth and had dragged her from her car toward the gray van.

The image of that dilapidated van was now sharp in her vision. The van. The man. He was driving her somewhere. But where? To her death? To an unspeakable horror that was too painful even to think about?

She could hold back no longer. Panic overwhelmed her as she realized that her fate was in the hands of a stranger whose motives were unknown. She was trapped in a situation that was out of her control.

Elizabeth tried to scream, but through the gag over her mouth, the sound she made was little more than a mournful gurgle.

Mercifully she passed out again.

Max Dellon had been staring at the page so long that the words had blurred into a mass of unreadable black ink. He had no idea what he'd been reading. Although the book was written in English—it was Shakespeare's *Othello*—for all he'd been able to understand, it might have been written in another language.

"Sir, he is rash and very sudden in choler and haply with his truncheon may strike at you." Max read the words again and shook his head in confusion. No one he knew talked like that. He felt it was terribly unfair of Mr. Collins to expect him to know what it meant, let alone why Iago bothered to say it in the first place.

Liz better get here right now, he told himself as he rubbed his eyes for what had to be the hundredth time that evening. He sneaked another glance at the digital clock perched on his amplifier. Seven o'clock. He could have sworn Elizabeth had told him she'd be over a little after six. Then again he could have heard wrong. It wouldn't have been the first time he'd gotten his signals crossed.

Max sat up on the sofa in the basement, which had been set up like a mini-studio, moved his eyes a little to the right, and stared longingly at the twelve-string Telecaster electric guitar leaning against the amplifier. He wanted to play so badly it hurt, but he didn't dare go anywhere near it. The last thing he needed was more trouble.

Things were bad enough. Besides constant complaints about his longish hair, messy room, and "attitude," Max's father had found another reason to get on his case—his music. Now he was in more trouble than ever before in his sixteen-and-a-half years.

It had started, in a small way, two years before, when he and Guy Chesney had gotten together every Saturday morning to fool around, with Max on guitar, Guy on keyboards. Gradually the sessions extended to Sunday and then into weekdays, and soon they'd hooked up with Dan Scott, a bass guitarist, Emily Mayer, a drummer, and Dana Larson, who could belt out a tune better than any other singer at Sweet Valley High. Their band, The Droids, got tighter and tighter, and for a while they were even playing club dates besides the parties and school dances they were hired for on a regular basis.

Somehow Max had been able to juggle the group with schoolwork—that is, until this term. The courses were tougher and the workload heavier. But no course was as rough for him as Mr. Collins's English class. Max hadn't been able to get a handle on any of the assignments all semester, particularly Shakespeare. He'd stopped listening to the lectures long ago and resigned himself to flunking the course, and making up the work in summer school.

It all made sense to Max. School was just a place to spend the time between late-night sessions playing with The Droids. He never said much in his classes, except to make up excuses for not having done his homework. Almost all his instructors had given him lots of warnings and angry glares, all of which were easy for Max to ignore.

But he couldn't disregard Mr. Collins. The English teacher hadn't been content just to warn Max; he had gone one step further and had contacted his parents, telling them that unless Max shaped up in a big way, he was going to fail. The key would be how he fared with *Othello*.

Roger Collins's message was all Max's father needed. He hadn't been happy at all with the late hours Max kept and the loud music coming from the basement. He didn't see any reason to tolerate it any longer, not when it threatened to ruin Max's future. The night Mr. Collins had called, Mr. Dellon laid down the law. Max was forbidden to play with the group until his grades picked up, and if he failed English, he'd have to give up the band for good. Max thought it was cruel of his father to cut him off from his music, but Mr. Dellon felt his son had been asking for it.

Despite the punishment, Max had been unable to help his own cause. He'd failed all the spot quizzes Mr. Collins had given on the play so far. That hadn't been surprising, considering that he couldn't get past act one, scene one. This test was his last chance. The big day was Monday, just two days away, and the only way he'd make it was with a tutor. That's where Elizabeth came in—or was supposed to.

Max was disturbed. It wasn't like Elizabeth to miss an appointment. What could be keeping her? He put down his copy of *Othello* and ambled up the staircase to the living room, where his parents were watching television. He stuck his head into the room. "Have you heard anything from Liz?" he asked.

His father looked up and scowled. "No. And get back downstairs and read that stuff over until she gets here. That's an order."

"Yes, sir." Scowling back, Max clicked his heels and gave his father a military salute.

"That's enough, Max. Get back to those books!"

Max stormed off, slamming the basement door behind him so hard the house shook. It was bad enough having to spend Saturday night at home, but having to take his father on top of it was driving him crazy.

Back downstairs, Max started to thumb through the *Cliff Notes* he'd picked up at the mall that afternoon. At least *they* were written in understandable English.

By eight o'clock, however, Max was no closer to understanding the play. He needed Elizabeth desperately.

Deciding he deserved another break, Max padded upstairs to the phone. His worry over his academic survival was now mixed with genuine concern over Elizabeth's whereabouts. He dialed her number but wasn't surprised when there was no answer. Elizabeth had told him she'd be coming straight from the hospital. But she should have been finished with that hours ago. *It doesn't feel right*, Max thought to himself as he returned to the basement. *Something must have happened to her. A flat tire. A family emergency.*

By nine-forty Max concluded that further study would be a waste of effort. He was much too worried about Elizabeth to do anything but stare senselessly at the words before him. He tried once more to call her house, but there was still no answer.

What if she was in trouble? Elizabeth, whom

everyone could always count on if he or she needed someone to talk to; Elizabeth, whose first-class reviews of The Droids in the Sweet Valley High paper had helped make Max's band the most popular one at school. Didn't he owe it to her to make sure she was OK? *I can't stay here any longer*, he decided. *I've got to try to find her.* But telling his parents would be a waste of time. They'd never let him go. Max again retreated to the basement, this time with no intention of staying. Quietly he let himself out the back door and headed toward the motorcycle parked alongside the house, the side away from the living room. Feeling a little like a criminal, Max pushed his bike across to the edge of the lawn and out into the street. He continued to walk beside the vehicle until he got around the corner. Then, when he was far enough away to avoid being heard and arousing the suspicions of his parents, he started it up. Without wasting another second, he took off in the direction of Fowler Memorial Hospital to search for Elizabeth.

Four

It was only nine o'clock, yet the night was already a success in Jessica's book—a success way beyond her expectations. She'd had an exclusive on nearly all Nicholas's attention so far, and for once she hadn't had to resort to her usual tricks to get it. All she had to do was answer Nicholas's questions about herself and about life in Sweet Valley.

She'd asked him plenty of questions about himself, too. She'd learned he'd graduated the previous June from an exclusive boarding school in Connecticut and was taking time off to study his father's computer business before heading to college. He was excited about the move to Sweet Valley, yet admitted his homesickness for the friends and memories he'd left behind in the East. Fortunately there were no girls in his past, at least no important ones. Jessica had managed to find that out right away. If things continued to go according to her plan, she'd make Nicholas forget about the East Coast in a hurry.

Nicholas excused himself for a moment to check on how the other guests were doing. He promised to be right back. As he walked away, Jessica spotted Caroline Pearce walking over. *Oh, no,* thought Jessica, turning abruptly on her heel, *not Miss Nosy of the Year herself.* But before Jessica had a chance to make her getaway, Caroline pushed her way through the crowd and came up behind her.

"Oh, Jessica, I just adore your dress," she gushed. As usual, Caroline was the picture of respectability, her pink shirtwaist dress buttoned right up to the collar, her red hair clipped back neatly. But for someone who was Miss Prim and Proper on the outside, Caroline had a nasty, gossipy streak. Even Elizabeth, who could find something nice to say about almost everyone, steered clear of Caroline.

"And I see Nicholas likes your outfit, too," Caroline said suggestively.

Jessica had no intention of giving Caroline the information she was digging for. "You look divine yourself," she said with studied sweetness.

40

She hoped Caroline would make a fast exit before Nicholas returned. Thinking quickly, she added, "You know, Caroline, pink is Winston Egbert's favorite color on a girl."

"Really?" Caroline stood a little straighter. She'd been interested in the gangly boy for quite some time but had no idea how to catch him.

"Sure," Jessica went on. "Haven't you seen the way he's been looking at you all evening?" It was a lie, of course. At that moment, Winston was heading, along with some of the others, to the swimming pool. "If I were you, I'd make sure I didn't let him out of my sight."

Caroline searched around the room. "I don't see him," she wailed.

Jessica pointed to the next room. "He went thataway."

Caroline beamed as if Jessica had just given her a million dollars. "Thanks, Jess. You're a doll!"

"Don't mention it," Jessica said as Caroline left. *Especially to Winston*, she thought with amusement. Like almost everyone else at Sweet Valley, Winston thought Caroline was creepy.

Jessica's timing was nothing if not perfect, for just then Nicholas came back. "Sorry for the delay," he said. "I got into a conversation with Bruce Patman."

"Bruce? I didn't know anyone from the senior class was here," Jessica said. "I thought this party was for juniors—present company excepted."

"Well, because he's our next-door neighbor, Regina figured she'd invite him. Not a bad guy. He saw me talking to you. Said you were one of the most interesting girls in town."

"Oh, really?" Jessica perked up. She and Bruce were not exactly on the best terms. She hoped he'd been a gentleman and hadn't soured Nicholas on her. "He's quite a fascinating guy himself," she said diplomatically.

Nicholas grinned, showing off the cleft in his chin. "I suppose you want to know what he said. Let me see if I can remember his exact words. . . . 'There is no such thing as having a dull time with Jessica.' Did you two have a thing going?"

"A long time ago," Jessica said, brushing aside her past love life. "Tell me, did you two make plans to race?"

"Race what?"

"Your cars, of course. Isn't that your Ferrari parked outside? It's a 308/GT, right? I've never been in one of those, but I understand they really fly."

"They do, but my experience is only as a passenger."

"That's not your car?"

Nicholas shook his head. "It's my father's. I'm not into flashy cars. I drive a good old reliable Jeep. But maybe I ought to get Bruce together with Regina. She'd love to race him."

"So Regina is the spitfire of the family?"

"She's really not allowed to drive, but Dad taught her anyway. He lets her take the car out on deserted roads. It makes my mother crazy. But Regina has a will of her own—" Nicholas was cut off in midsentence as a tall, dark-haired boy approached them and tapped Jessica on the shoulder.

Annoyed, Jessica turned around, ready to pounce on the intruder.

It was Todd Wilkins, Elizabeth's boyfriend. On the best of occasions they barely got along; Jessica tolerated him only for her sister's sake. She couldn't imagine what great calamity was making him bother her now, of all times.

Todd wasn't thrilled about interrupting Jessica either. But he felt he had no choice. He had spent the past half hour combing the grounds for Elizabeth and couldn't find her anywhere. He knew she and Jessica were supposed to have come to the party together. Ordinarily he would have picked up Elizabeth himself, but with her tight time schedule she'd thought it would be easier if he just met her at the party.

43

"Jessica, excuse me for bothering you, but—"

Facing him with an icy stare, Jessica blurted out, "Not now, Todd. Whatever it is can wait. Can't it?"

"No, it can't, Jess," Todd said firmly. He grabbed Jessica's arm. But before Todd could get a response from her, Nicholas jerked his hand away. "Just what do you think you're doing?" Nicholas asked angrily. "She doesn't want you around."

Ignoring Nicholas's menacing glare, Todd turned back to Jessica. "Do you know where Liz is? I'm worried."

A look of concern flitted across Jessica's perfect features, and she felt that strange little shiver run through her body again. Maybe she should try to find out what was keeping her sister. But out of the corner of her eye, she spotted rich and beautiful Lila Fowler staring at Nicholas and her. Ever since she'd arrived, Lila had been trailing him like a bloodhound in search of prey, and Jessica knew Lila would pounce on Nicholas the moment she stepped away. Besides, her sister was most likely back home in the shower at that very moment. Just because Todd worried needlessly about the silliest things didn't mean she had to get all worked up, too. The important thing was to get him out of her hair. If she told him the truth, that she didn't exactly know where her twin was, Todd might continue to press her and further interrupt her and Nicholas. No, the truth wouldn't do.

"I'm sorry, Todd," she said, the sweetness back in her voice. "I thought Liz had told you, but I guess she couldn't get through to you in time. Mr. Collins called right before she went to the hospital. Something came up, some important school function he found out he had to go to at the last minute. He asked her to baby-sit Teddy for an hour or two, and you know Liz, she couldn't say no. She ought to be here soon."

"Are you sure, Jess?"

Jessica cocked her head and shot Todd a look of pure indignation. "Now why would I lie about something like that?"

Todd shook his head. "Sorry to have bothered you." He walked off toward Elizabeth's best friend, Enid Rollins, but his thoughts were a million miles away from the party. His encounter with Jessica hadn't eased his mind at all. Something about her story didn't make sense, yet he had no concrete reason to doubt her. It wasn't like Jessica to lie where Elizabeth was concerned. Despite their differences, the one thing he and Jessica shared was their love for Elizabeth. If something had happened to her, the last thing in the world Jessica would do would be to party up a storm.

But Todd couldn't make the doubt go away. Still, there was nothing he could do now except wait until Elizabeth finally showed up.

Five

When Elizabeth came to again, the first thing she became aware of was the cold. Not a searing wind, but cool wisps of air that felt as if they were seeping through tiny holes in the wall of wherever she'd been taken. She sensed she was no longer in the van. There was no movement underneath her, and the dank smell she remembered had been replaced with the pungent odor of old garbage and fried food. But it was impossible for her to tell where she was. She was still blindfolded, gagged, and tied—and more terrified than she'd ever been in her life.

At least she was still alive.

She was in no pain, but her head felt a little heavy from whatever had made her pass out. Some kind of drug-soaked rag had been clamped over her nose and mouth, she recalled. But the memory of her actual abduction was still hazy.

None of that was important, however. What mattered most was where she was now and what was to become of her. Now that the cool air was helping to clear her head, she had to try to get away. Her hands were still tied together with rope, and as she moved she realized the rest of her body was also tied down. The chair she was sitting on scraped against a bare wooden floor as she struggled to break free. For a few minutes she tugged frantically at the ropes, hoping the friction would help untangle them. But it was useless; the ties refused to budge.

She tried to scream, but her cries were muffled by the gag. Where was she? What was going to happen to her?

Elizabeth felt herself becoming frantic as the questions mounted in her mind. She had no idea how long she'd been there or how long it had been since she was brutally pulled away from her car. Or even if anyone knew she was missing. With the limited movement allowed her she tried to get a sense of herself. A gentle shake of her head told her that her hair was still pulled back in a braid. Then, pressing her bound hands against her body, she concluded that she was still wearing her uniform. Its relative crispness indicated that she hadn't been unconscious too long—a couple of hours, maybe, but not days.

Who would do this to her? And why? She struggled to think of someone who might have a reason to harm her, but she couldn't. Yet Elizabeth couldn't quell the nagging sensation that it had been someone she knew. She had a feeling she'd seen him, too, before she passed out, but his image was now blocked from her mind. It was maddening, reminding her of the time after her motorcycle accident when she'd temporarily forgotten her own identity. To know that she knew something but couldn't transfer it from the subconscious to the conscious—

She heard a car speed by somewhere in the distance, its brakes squealing as it rounded a corner. Elizabeth strained her ears to hear more, but she picked up nothing immediate, nothing to indicate she was close to any houses. Or people. Or help.

Elizabeth's eyes began to moisten under the cloth bandage that was keeping them shut. At this moment she should have been laughing and dancing and having fun at Regina Morrow's party, not shivering in this dark, eerie room; not tied up, helpless and scared; not trying to hold back the refrain that was repeating itself over and over in her brain like a nightmarish tape she couldn't turn off: *What's to become of me? Am I going to die? Am I going to die?*

Suddenly she heard the crunch of tires moving across dirt and stone, accompanied by the rumble of a vehicle badly in need of a tune-up. Then the motor stopped, and a few seconds later a door slammed shut. It sounded close, as if it were right outside the building she was in.

Elizabeth flinched. Her kidnapper had come back. She didn't know what felt worse, the awful fear of not knowing what was going on or the stark realization that she would find out in just a few moments.

Moments that could be the last of her life.

Elizabeth heard the heavy, plodding footsteps outside pause momentarily as a key jiggled in the lock on what she assumed was the front door. When the door opened and then slammed shut, Elizabeth felt another wave of cold penetrate her entire being. This time it wasn't the night air, but the cold sweat of unmitigated fear.

"Help!" she tried to scream through the gag.

The man continued to walk across the room.

"Help!" she screamed again.

The man must have heard her muffled cries that time. His heavy footsteps grew louder and more menacing with each approaching step. Then he was there, right in front of her, his shoes toe to toe with Elizabeth's trembling feet.

Elizabeth began to pray. She realized that this could be the end. She tried to steel herself for the worst. Since there was nothing she could do to stop him, she hoped he would get it over with quickly and not torture her first. That is, not torture her physically. These last few minutes had been mental torture that was almost too much to bear.

In the darkness she sensed his hand approaching her head. To strangle her? Knock her senseless? Or, by some miracle, remove her bindings?

"Stop. Please stop! I don't want to die!" Her muffled words were the only defense she could muster.

What the man did next was something Elizabeth couldn't believe. Gently he ran his thick, stubby fingers across her hair and then unwound her braid, slowly, methodically, until her soft blond hair fell to her shoulders. Then he caressed the strands and whispered, "It's all right. I'm not going to hurt you. Everything's going to be fine."

Though Elizabeth couldn't quite place it, his voice sounded vaguely familiar. But his words did little to calm her fears. She had no reason to trust him. There was every chance that he was lying or that his tender handling of her hair was a prelude to violence. She remained rigid in the chair, every muscle tense with fear.

"I see you don't believe me," the man continued. "I guess I understand, but it was the only way I could think of to bring you here, Elizabeth."

He knows my name! While her brain registered

that revelation, she struggled to identify the voice. It didn't sound like someone from school. He sounded older, possibly someone she knew from the hospital since that was where she was kidnapped. "Who are you? Where am I?" Again her words were muffled, and the man said nothing.

He didn't answer with words. In the same slow, methodical way he had untied her braid, the man unraveled the cloth that had kept her eyes in darkness. When it was removed, even the lone, bare light bulb that dimly lit the room stung her eyes, and it took Elizabeth a few seconds to focus on her captor.

Oh, God! It was Carl, the sad-looking, lonely hospital orderly. Then everything that had happened came rushing back. She remembered now, remembered when Carl had tricked her into getting out of her car and pressed a handkerchief full of chloroform to her face. Then she had sunk into unconsciousness.

Carl. Whom she sensed had been following her around the hospital ever since she had started working there. Carl. The man who always seemed to gaze at her with a strange sense of longing. Carl. The man whose actions had disturbed her lately.

But not enough to report him—or even to share her concerns with anyone else. Now it was too late.

Elizabeth began to cry. If she'd told someone—anyone—about her suspicions, this terrible nightmare might never have happened. Yet she'd resisted reporting him because she'd felt sorry for the man. Although he was about twenty-five, his attitude made him seem younger to Elizabeth—he appeared so alone and so vulnerable. She'd come to his rescue once, when she'd helped him pick up a tray of supplies he'd dropped. He was so grateful to her, as if she alone had helped save him from being fired. She'd had no desire to get him in trouble, even though he did seem peculiar and his staring had made her uncomfortable.

If only I weren't so trusting! she thought, still terrified of what Carl might do. Knowing who her abductor was hadn't changed a thing. She shivered again. She didn't know him well at all, and it didn't take much stretching of her imagination to conclude that someone who was capable of drugging and kidnapping her might do anything!

At the moment, however, he didn't seem ready to kill her. Carl was kneeling in front of her now, his dark, deep-set eyes filled with the sadness he seemed always to carry around with him. Elizabeth decided to play on that sadness. Surely Carl would feel worse with a murder victim on his hands. Elizabeth looked at him with moistened eyes and pleaded silently for him to spare her life.

He seemed to read her thoughts. "I promise I'm not going to hurt you," he repeated.

But you are hurting me, Elizabeth thought, her tears soaking her gag. She still had no idea how long she'd been there, but the ropes on her hands and feet were irritating her, and her muscles ached from being forced to sit in what she now saw was an old, splintery wooden chair. She wiggled as much as she could to show her discomfort.

Carl nodded, his eyes dropping to the bare floor. "I understand. The ties. I can't let you loose yet. But if it will make you more comfortable, I'll remove the gag."

As soon as he did, Elizabeth released a blood-curdling scream. "Help me! For God's sake someone help me!"

Six

It had been half an hour since Jessica had given him the brush-off, and Todd still couldn't shake his uneasiness about Elizabeth. Jessica's story just didn't gel. It seemed to him that his girlfriend would have had plenty of opportunities to tell him about her change of plans. He'd been home all evening before the party, and the phone hadn't rung once.

Maybe he should call her at Mr. Collins's and put his fears to rest. Elizabeth would certainly understand his concern, and besides, the call would give Todd a better idea of when he could expect her to arrive. He wasn't enjoying this party without her.

Todd remembered seeing a telephone in the foyer. Before leaving the den, however, his eyes momentarily locked with Enid's. He hadn't said a word to her about Elizabeth, but in that one look he could see the troubled expression in Enid's green eyes. She was worried about her friend too.

Todd dialed quickly, anticipating the sound of Elizabeth's cheerful "hello." The phone was answered after two rings, but by a deep voice. A man's voice.

"Mr. Collins!" Todd didn't try to hide his surprise. "I didn't think you'd be there."

"Why not? I live here. Now who is this?" he said. He sounded perplexed.

"Oh, I'm sorry. It's me, Todd Wilkins. Can I speak to Elizabeth, please?"

"Liz? What makes you think she's here?"

"Isn't she baby-sitting for you?"

"No, Todd. What gave you that idea?"

Todd would have gladly strangled Jessica then and there. He didn't know what her game was, why she'd misled him, but he was furious. He tried to keep his voice calm as he said to Mr. Collins, "It must have been a misunderstanding. I'm sorry to have bothered you."

Roger Collins was still holding the phone after Todd hung up. He hoped Elizabeth was OK. He shook his head as he replaced the receiver. Sometimes being a teacher at Sweet Valley High seemed like a twenty-four-hour-a-day job.

Meanwhile, with a sense of impending doom, Todd ran back to the den and scanned the group frantically for Jessica. She wasn't there. He found her moments later by the pool, sitting at the edge of the deep end, clad in a skimpy nothing of a bikini. Her feet skimmed the water as she leaned back casually on her arms. She was deep in conversation with Nicholas Morrow.

But not for long. Todd went up to her from behind, and without thinking twice, gave her a smooth shove, right into the water.

She surfaced a moment later, her hair plastered around her face like a golden helmet. With venom in her eyes, she glared at Todd. "You idiot!" she screamed. "I'm going to kill you!"

"Which is what I should have done to you," Todd countered ferociously. "You got off easy, Jessica."

Nicholas came to her defense. Rising from the pool's edge, he grabbed Todd's arm and held it in a viselike grip. Although Nicholas was several inches shorter than Todd, he had no trouble containing the angry boy. "What's your problem, Todd?" he asked through clenched teeth. "This is the second time tonight you've bothered that poor girl. I'm going to have to ask you to leave."

"Don't bother. I'm on my way out. But I've got to set a few things straight first." He turned back to Jessica, who was still treading water. "Do you have any idea what time it is?"

Jessica thought Todd was the one who'd gone off the deep end. "I don't know, and I don't care. I don't even own a watch."

Todd kneeled down at the water's edge. "Jess," he said, his eyes pleading for her to listen, "I'm worried sick about Liz. I know she didn't go to Mr. Collins. It's after nine-thirty. She should have been here over an hour ago!"

"Nine-thirty. I hadn't realized. . . ." Jessica's voice trailed off as she finally understood what Todd was driving at. A sense of déjà vu overwhelmed her, and the vision made her shudder despite the heated water. Her mind replayed the horrible night of Elizabeth's motorcycle accident, a night that had been the most frightening of Jessica's life.

Jessica had promised Elizabeth a ride from the party they'd attended that night, but she'd forgotten all about it in her mad chase after Enid's cousin Brian. Elizabeth had had to take a lift on Todd's motorcycle, which her parents had forbidden her to ride. Then came the accident, which Jessica was certain never would have happened if she'd kept her word.

Now, she'd done it again. The Fiat had been acting a little cranky lately. For all she knew, Elizabeth could be stranded on a lonely road at that very moment while she was busy homing in on yet another conquest.

Jessica jumped out of the water. "Todd, we've got to find her!" Her concern was mounting with each passing second. She turned to Nicholas, who had already loosened his hold on Todd. "Where's the phone? I've got to make a call!"

Ned and Alice Wakefield were laughing heartily as they walked up the path to their house. "You can't say Doug is the shy, retiring type," Elizabeth's mother said. She was referring to her new business associate, who'd taken them out to dinner.

"But you never told me what a comedian he was," Mr. Wakefield said as he turned the lock on the front door. "I don't remember the last time I laughed so hard. He didn't stop telling jokes all evening."

"Only to order dinner," Mrs. Wakefield corrected, holding up a white paper bag in her right hand, "except he shouldn't have ordered such large steaks for us. There's enough left over here for sandwiches tomorrow." She lowered her voice and added, "For the two of us, that is."

Mr. Wakefield took off his topcoat and headed toward the hall closet. "I don't think the kids will mind," he said. "The girls usually fend for themselves on Sundays anyway."

"I'm going to put this in the refrigerator. I'll be right back," Mrs. Wakefield said. Still wearing her stylish suede jacket, she walked through the dining room toward the kitchen.

She switched on the light and put the doggie bag on the bottom shelf of the refrigerator, pushing the door closed with the edge of her boot heel. Then, leaning against the kitchen table, she combed her fingers through her golden hair—and mentally ran through all the things she planned to get done the following day.

A folded piece of paper on the table caught her eye. Moments later her brow furrowed as she read its contents. "Ned," she called out. "Come in here, would you?"

A smile brightening his handsome, tanned face, the twins' father sauntered casually into the room. "Surprising me with a nightcap?" He locked arms with his wife, a gesture that Alice Wakefield almost always found comforting, even after twenty years of marriage.

But not this time. "I'm worried, Ned," she said, holding out the note Jessica had written for her sister.

Mr. Wakefield didn't see a problem. "Looks like standard operating procedure around here to me," he said after reading it. "Jessica asking

Liz to do her a favor, then changing her plans at the last minute."

Alice Wakefield shook her head. "But this note was still folded when I came in. I don't think Liz ever saw it. I don't think she came home."

"Did you realize you get these cute little lines around your mouth when you get upset?"

Mrs. Wakefield slumped down in a chair. "Cut it out, Ned. I'm serious."

"I am, too," he said, cupping his hands on her shoulders. He began to massage the growing tension out of his wife's back. "I can think of a hundred reasons why Liz wouldn't see the note, and ninety-nine of them are no cause for worry."

She wasn't relieved. "I'm listening," she said, turning the paper over and over in her hands.

Ned Wakefield hesitated. "Well, Liz could have gone straight to the party from the hospital—"

"No, she had that tutoring session tonight."

"Right. So she could have gone straight from there. Or she could have come through the front door and not seen it. Or even walked right by it and ignored it completely." He took the note away from his wife. "It wasn't the smartest place to leave a message. Jessica should have known better."

"Well, counselor, what you say makes sense,

but I think I'd feel a little better if we called the Morrows and made sure the girls were there."

"And have them think we're checking up on them? You're the victim of an overactive imagination, Alice. I'm sure everything's fine. Come on, let's go upstairs."

Reluctantly Mrs. Wakefield followed her husband out of the kitchen. He was right, she tried to convince herself. She was being overly sensitive and jumping to conclusions. It was a pattern she'd fallen into in recent months. Ever since Elizabeth had had that terrible accident, Alice Wakefield had been fighting a compulsion to monitor her daughter's every movement. Not that she'd made Elizabeth aware of this. On a rational level Mrs. Wakefield knew her daughter was responsible and mature enough not to need a mother's protection. Her maternal instincts had caused her to pay closer attention to Elizabeth's schedule anyway. Without appearing to pry, she had been able to pretty much keep tabs on where Elizabeth was at any given hour of the day. She found herself fighting a strong urge to phone the Morrows now.

The Wakefields were halfway up the stairs to their bedroom when the phone rang.

"Daddy, is that you?" Jessica's words came out in a rush. "It's me, Jess. I'm at the Morrows. Is Liz there?"

Mr. Wakefield felt a lump form in his throat.

He drew his hand up to it as if to clear it away before speaking. "You mean she isn't there?"

Upon hearing her husband's side of the conversation, Mrs. Wakefield clasped his hand tightly. She let out an anguished gasp as she realized all her worst fears might be justified. Her husband pulled her toward him, holding her close.

"She never showed up, Daddy," Jessica said as Nicholas thoughtfully placed an oversize bath towel around her shivering body. "I'm worried."

"Don't be, princess. I'm sure your sister is fine. But your mother and I would feel better if you came home now."

"I'm on my way anyway. Todd's going to bring me. But if you don't mind, we're going to drive up and down the streets first. Liz's car might have broken down."

"Good idea, Jess. I'll call the hospital in the meantime. She may have decided to work late." Mr. Wakefield tried to sound reassuring, but he didn't think his daughter would believe that any more than he did.

"Bye, Daddy."

Jessica dropped the phone frantically and turned to Todd. "Come on, let's go." Without bothering to change or get her coat, Jessica hurried through the maze of people to the front entrance. Todd nearly broke into a full run to keep up with her.

Nicholas brought up the rear and got to the foyer just in time to see the two of them closing the front door. "I'll keep in touch," he called out. But it was unlikely that Jessica heard him.

She was already berating herself. It was stupid, stupid of her to have concocted that silly story about the baby-sitting job. It was totally unnecessary. It hadn't done anyone any good. It had made no difference to her budding relationship with Nicholas. She'd had to run out on him anyway; and now he knew she had lied about Elizabeth.

At what cost? she wondered bitterly as Todd pulled around the circular driveway and out the gates of the Morrow estate. *Is Nicholas—or any guy?—worth the possibility of losing my sister?*

"No!" she wailed aloud, breaking the silence in Todd's car.

Todd was still furious with her, though discretion had forced him to say nothing up to that point. But he couldn't hold back any longer. Gripping his steering wheel in a white-knuckled clench, he spat out. "Was it worth it, Jessica?"

Tears were flowing down her face. She knew Todd had a right to be angry with her. "Say it, Todd. Say anything you want about me. Believe me, whatever it is, it can't be as bad as what I'm thinking. I'll never forgive myself if something's happened to Liz. I know you think

I'm just saying that, but I mean it, Todd. I really do."

Out of the corner of his eye, Todd could see her tears were genuine. While he wouldn't put it past Jessica to engage in a bout of feeling sorry for herself in an attempt to get pity, he wanted to believe she was sincere this time. The only person or thing Jessica truly couldn't live without was her twin, and Todd knew she would fall to pieces if something were to happen to Elizabeth.

He decided not to press the matter of why she had lied to him. Instead, he looked past her tears and, for the first time since they left, realized she was practically naked. She was shivering, tightly clutching the towel that covered her shoulders. "You forgot to change."

Jessica shrugged. "There was no time."

"There's time for this." Holding the steering wheel with one arm and then the other, Todd wiggled out of his leather jacket and held it out for Jessica to take. "Here, put it on."

Jessica remained where she was, clutching the towel. "No."

Todd's eyes widened in surprise. "What do you mean, no?"

"I deserve to get pneumonia after what I did to Liz this evening."

"Oh, come on, Jess. That wouldn't help anyone," he said, his tone softening. He glanced at Jessica. Her face was so full of concern that for the briefest moment he imagined it was Elizabeth next to him and not her identical twin. *Jessica really does love her sister more than anyone in the world*, thought Todd. Gently he reached over and placed the jacket over her shoulders. *Maybe if we work as a team—just this once,* Todd told himself, *we'll be able to bring Elizabeth home safe and sound.*

Seven

Carl clamped his hand over Elizabeth's mouth and muffled her scream. "What'd you have to go and do that for?" he asked. But he didn't expect an answer. With his other hand he pushed up on her jaw and held her mouth closed. The pressure hurt her, and seeing that it would be futile to continue screaming, she stopped.

When Carl was sure she was finished, he let go of her jaw. Continuing to kneel in front of her, he repeated "It's OK" over and over as if he were chanting.

As he waited for her to calm down and stop shaking, he studied her as if she were a museum piece. "Why did you scream?" he asked again, his gentle voice in marked contrast to the force he'd just exerted. He didn't seem angry, just terribly confused.

"I'm scared," she replied. She pronounced each word slowly, calmly, as she tried to get hold of herself. "I don't want to be here."

"You will," he said, his voice turning friendly. "In time you're going to be grateful I brought you here. I'll make sure you do."

Elizabeth didn't know what to make of that. "How?" she asked timidly.

"By being nice to you."

The words were so ordinary, something she'd expect a boy to say on a first date. It didn't make sense for Carl to talk to her like that. Elizabeth was too confused to respond.

Carl looked around. He seemed slightly nervous himself and was running the gag back and forth through his fingers. "Don't be afraid of me. I'm not going to hurt you."

Elizabeth looked at the gag warily. "Are you going to put that back in my mouth?" she asked.

"No," he said.

The answer surprised her. "Aren't you afraid I might scream again?"

He shook his head. "I guess it wouldn't make any difference anyway. Nobody around here would care—not that there's much chance of anyone hearing you."

"Why not? Where are we? Where have you taken me?"

"Calm down, Elizabeth. You're safe now." He stood up and waved his arms in a proud gesture. "Welcome to my house."

Elizabeth took her first good look at her new surroundings. There wasn't much to see. In better times the room she was in might have been a living room, but now it was little more than a dingy, nearly empty space about the size of her bedroom. To her left was the front door, and against the wall in front of her was a torn, floral-print sofa. Straining her neck she caught a glimpse of a table and another chair similar to the one she was tied to, which, like the sofa, looked like Salvation Army rejects. Behind her and to the right was a stove, then an archway, which she thought probably led to the bathroom and perhaps a bedroom. The lone window on the wall next to the door was boarded over with planks of weathered wood, and the floor was worn and stained with grime. The walls were dirty, too, and there were no pictures or any kind of personal mementos that Elizabeth would have expected to see in a place someone called home.

"Where are we?" she repeated.

"My house," he said again, adding, "though I want you to start thinking of it as your house, too."

My house? Elizabeth shuddered with revulsion. She couldn't imagine ever growing accustomed

69

to this hovel. "How long do you plan to keep me here?"

Carl smiled. "Forever."

The pronouncement made Elizabeth snap her eyes shut. Everything was happening so quickly. But the facts were becoming clear. A few minutes earlier she had been staring at death, and now she faced the prospect of spending the rest of her life with Carl. She didn't know which was worse.

She forced herself to open her eyes again and look at Carl, hoping to uncover the motive behind this madness. But his expression revealed little more than she already knew. His eyes were serious, with no hint of the wild-eyed or vacant stare she thought she'd see in someone mad enough to kidnap another person. The lines around his eyes and the way the corners of his mouth turned downward suggested something else too: the expression of overall sadness she remembered seeing at the hospital, a sadness she was at a loss to understand. "Why am I here?" she asked.

"Because I love you." His reply was quick, his voice almost childlike in its simple declaration—as if it were obvious.

Elizabeth couldn't believe he meant it. How could he? He didn't know anything about her. Or did he? Elizabeth reflected ruefully that he'd been able to find out what car she drove and when she got off work. How much had he learned by following her around the hospital?

She didn't know, and she didn't want to stay around long enough to find out. The only thing on her mind now was escape. She thought frantically of a plan as she scanned the room. The window was boarded up tightly, and she had to assume that windows in the back of the house were similarly secured. But the door was held closed with only one lock and a chain. She would need only a few seconds to get through those barriers. But to do it, she'd have to divert Carl's attention. It would be difficult, as she doubted he'd let her out of his sight, but she had to try.

No plan to escape could get started, however, until she got Carl to untie her. But when she asked him to do so his reply was, "Not yet."

Elizabeth had no answer, and she remained silent for a moment. Then an obvious solution came to mind. "Carl," she said, trying hard to make her voice sound sweet, "I have to go to the bathroom."

For a second he looked confused, as if that were a possibility he hadn't planned on when he tied her to the chair. Then his face relaxed. "OK," he said. Coming around to the back of the chair, he removed the bonds strapped around her body.

To Elizabeth's surprise she smiled, grateful to

71

have even this much freedom of movement. Almost as a reflex, the first thing she did was bend forward, touching her head to her knees to get the kinks out of her back. It felt so good to move again. But even more important, she knew that every muscle in her body must work properly if she was to escape.

But Carl had a surprise for her—he didn't untie everything. After she straightened herself up in the chair, he pulled her into a standing position, with her hands and feet still tied together. Then he scooped her up in his arms and carried her toward the bathroom door, behind the archway. He put her back on her feet, and only then did he remove her bonds, keeping a firm grasp on her until she was inside the closet-sized room. Then he closed the door swiftly behind her. Carl had taken no risks when he untied her, for it was impossible to escape from this windowless cell.

But at least he's giving me privacy, Elizabeth said to herself while Carl waited outside for her. With her freedom taken away, she realized that any victory, no matter how small, was to be cherished. If she'd done nothing else, she had at least succeeded in getting away from that chair. And what was more, she could move about unrestrained. She swung her arms around to get her circulation going and flexed her legs, marveling at how wonderful these simple motions could feel. She stayed in the bathroom as long as she could, until Carl started knocking on the door. Then, knowing it would do no good to fight, Elizabeth emerged and allowed him to retie her.

As he carried her back into the living room, she turned to him and asked, "Could I sit on the sofa now?" Her eyes were a sea of hope.

Carl shrugged. "I don't see why not."

The sofa was too soft and lumpy, but compared to the chair, it felt luxurious. From this vantage point she could see the rest of the house —and it was just as drab as it had seemed before. Now she was able to examine the kitchen, a tiny room containing an ancient refrigerator, a hot plate, a chipped sink, and open shelves where cabinets should have been. Except for a couple of cheap plastic plates and a few cans, they were bare.

Elizabeth felt her stomach churn. The last thing she'd eaten had been a chocolate bar around four that afternoon. She was hungry. Very hungry. But she refused to ask Carl for something to eat. She didn't want to ask him for anything. She didn't want anything from him.

Except her freedom.

Carl had pulled up a chair and set up camp about a foot away from the sofa. He did and said nothing. The act of looking at Elizabeth was enough to keep a smile on his face. She was horribly disturbed by his continual ogling, but she tried not to show it, and for a while she said nothing.

She had to think. She'd counted on the bathroom ploy and was disappointed that it had failed. She wondered what she'd done wrong until she realized that Carl didn't trust her. *It must have been the scream*, she concluded. But that didn't get her very far. She had no idea how to make him trust her or whether she would be able to. Elizabeth believed that trust had to be earned, and that meant it would take time.

Time was something she didn't have.

She racked her brains desperately for a way to break free. And slowly a plan took shape. It was a long shot, but it might be her only chance. "Carl, can I ask you something?" He nodded, and then she continued, "Why do you love me?"

"Because you're kind. And because you like me."

"What makes you think I like you?"

"You're the only person in the hospital who cares about me."

"Are you talking about the time I helped you with the tray?"

The way Carl's face lit up just then made Elizabeth realize that their brief encounter was probably one of the happiest moments of his life. *How sad for him,* she thought, her heart beginning to go out to this pitiable man. Then she stopped the thought in its tracks. *This poor, pitiable guy has kidnapped you, you jerk! He's taken you away from everyone you know and love.* She hardened herself. She couldn't afford to have sympathy for him now, not with her own life on the line. She took a deep breath. She had to stay calm and carefully steer this discussion in exactly the right direction. It was her one hope for freedom.

"Carl," Elizabeth said, "I helped you that day because I like you." She forced herself to say the words. "I've always been nice to the people I like. What do you think about that? Do you want to be nice to me?"

"Yes," Carl answered, as if it were the most obvious thing in the world.

"Does that mean you don't want to hurt me?"

"I already told you that."

"How would you feel if you found out you're causing me pain?"

"Sad." Carl's gravelly voice shook a little.

"Would you want to do something about it?"

"Yes." Then, beginning to understand, he asked, "Are you in pain?"

"Yes, Carl." Elizabeth held out her hands. "These ropes hurt."

"But I was careful not to tie them too tight."

"Oh, I realize that, and I'm very grateful to you for being so considerate. But that doesn't change the fact that they hurt now. I can feel the ropes burning my skin. I'm going to have marks there, ugly red blotches. Do you really want to cause me pain?"

"Of course not, Elizabeth. I love you."

"Then could you take them off? From my hands and feet?"

"You'll leave me."

"No, I won't," Elizabeth promised.

"But you screamed at me."

"I'm sorry my screaming bothered you. I was afraid. I didn't know why you'd brought me here, and I thought you were going to hurt me."

"Oh, no, I wouldn't ever do that."

Elizabeth nodded insistently. "I know that now. I'm not afraid of you anymore. I like you, Carl. So won't you untie me, please?"

Carl didn't respond.

"I won't leave," she insisted. "Besides, where would I go? I have no idea where I am."

Carl said nothing for a long time. He seemed unsure what to do. Elizabeth took his hesitation as a hopeful sign that he was considering untying her—an act that would bring her one step closer to freedom.

Finally he spoke up, his voice full of hesitation. "Are—are you sure?"

"Of what?"

"Sure you won't leave me?"

"I already gave you my promise. I won't leave you, Carl." Inside Elizabeth was singing, her heart cautiously optimistic. *He's going to do it! He's going to do it!*

In her mind she planned her escape. Because he never left her side, she decided her only chance of success lay in the element of surprise. The moment Carl untied her she would bolt for the door. She was counting on his being momentarily stunned by her action for the few precious seconds she would need to undo the lock.

Elizabeth was still trembling inside, but she felt better now than she had since this ordeal began. Her plan of action gave her hope. She prayed she had the courage to carry it out and refused to dwell on what might happen if she failed. The possibilities were too frightening to contemplate.

Carl made good on his promise to Elizabeth— he wasn't going to let her remain in pain. Kneeling down on both knees, he untied the ropes around Elizabeth's hands. She felt the blood rush back into her palms. Silently Carl proceeded to her ankles and removed the ropes in a matter of seconds. Elizabeth watched him intently. This was her chance for escape!

As he gathered the rope in his hands, she

jumped up from the sofa and reached the door in less than three strides. Willing herself to steady her trembling fingers, she unfastened the chain lock as Carl became aware of what was happening.

"Elizabeth!" he cried as he rose to prevent her escape. "Elizabeth, no!"

She unlocked the bolt and opened the door that would lead to freedom. It wouldn't be long. Once outside, she was sure she'd be able to outrun the heavyset young man.

She gasped. In the split second before Carl seized her, she felt as if someone had plunged her into an ice-cold, vast, inescapable sea. She'd never had a chance. In that fleeting moment Elizabeth realized for the first time how utterly futile her plan had been.

Beyond the wooden door she'd opened was yet another door, some three feet in front of her, surrounded by an area that once might have been a screened-in porch but was now boarded up. There was no way she could have reached it in time.

Carl grabbed her under her arms and pushed her back to the sofa. Elizabeth didn't offer any resistance. He was much bigger and stronger than she, and to fight would have been useless. It would have served only to prove the awful truth: Carl was in total control. And there was nothing she could do to stop him.

It didn't look good for Elizabeth. Carl was furious at her and threw her onto the sofa with the force of a man possessed. His eyes now bright with anger, he came toward her.

This is it, thought Elizabeth as she squeezed her eyes shut. *This is the end.*

Eight

Jessica charged through the front door, followed by Todd, hoping against hope to find good news waiting for her. Their search up and down the streets of Sweet Valley had turned up no sign of Elizabeth, and by the time she and Todd pulled up in front of her house, they were both beginning to fear the worst.

Jessica found her parents in the living room. Her mother was pacing back and forth nervously, her anxiety evident in the creases that lined her forehead. Her father was on the phone, his expression one of fearful anticipation as he awaited news of his daughter.

"Mom!" Jessica ran into her mother's arms. "Have you heard anything yet?"

"No," her mother responded with a sigh,

pulling away from Jessica. "Your father's still on the phone with the hospital. Liz hasn't answered any of their pages, but someone's looking around for her now." Impulsively she reached for her daughter again and hugged her more tightly than at any time since Jessica was a baby. "I'm so glad you're home."

"Liz'll be all right, Mom," Jessica said, returning the hug. "Have you called Steve?"

Mrs. Wakefield shook her head. "He's got enough trouble of his own right now. No sense in worrying him further. Liz'll probably be back before he gets home anyway." She smiled hopefully for Jessica's sake. Then Alice Wakefield turned her attention to Todd, who was standing quietly at the entrance to the living room. "Hello, Todd. Why don't you come sit down," she invited.

"Thanks, Mrs. Wakefield," he said as he moved toward the sofa. "And don't worry. Liz'll probably be pulling into the driveway any second now."

No one really believed that, yet they all looked at each other with startled anticipation as they heard the motor of an approaching car a moment later.

But it continued past the house, the noise fading into the distance. *That's the second time tonight*, Jessica thought, remembering the headlights earlier in the evening that she had hoped would be her sister arriving home. *It's all my fault*, she told herself furiously. *If only I hadn't been so eager to get to that party, we might have had a head start on finding Elizabeth. She might be here right now.*

Jessica shivered in her still-damp suit, as much from fear as from cold.

Alice Wakefield noticed for the first time how little her daughter was wearing. "Jessica, get upstairs this minute and put some clothes on. You'll catch your death—" She swallowed the rest of the sentence, letting that ugly last word hang over the room like an invisible shroud. Everyone was thinking the same horrible thought, though no one dared say it out loud. The possibility was too terrible even to consider.

Mrs. Wakefield slumped down in a chair. "Go get dressed, Jessica," she repeated. Her voice was softer, her words almost a plea.

Silently Jessica slipped up the stairs and hastily threw on the first garments she could find, a Sweet Valley High T-shirt and a pair of sweat pants. She returned to the living room just as her father was hanging up the receiver.

"Nothing." Ned Wakefield let out a deep breath. "They looked all around the hospital and couldn't find her. One of the nurses thought she saw her leaving through the side entrance around six."

"She was going to Max Dellon's," Jessica said. "Have you tried him? She must be there. Yeah, that's it! She's still at Max's."

"I've been on with the hospital all this time," her father said. "He's next on my list." He'd already taken out the phone book and now was scanning the pages for the Dellon number.

"Max is having a really awful time of it in English. I'll bet you anything Liz insisted on staying there until she could drive some of that stuff into his head," Todd put in.

Mr. Wakefield dialed the number and asked for his daughter. A moment later his face fell. "They haven't seen her," he announced. "Max's mother says he has been down in their basement studying all evening. It's possible that she went in through the downstairs entrance. Mrs. Dellon's going to check." Tensely they awaited the response.

The two or three minutes Max's mother was gone from the phone were like an eternity to the Wakefield family. "I see. Yes, thank you Mrs. Dellon." Mr. Wakefield put down the phone and tried to keep his voice steady. "She looked all over. Max isn't there." His voice began to choke. "And neither is Elizabeth."

"Maybe they went someplace together," Jessica said hopefully.

Her father shook his head. "Mr. Dellon went

outside to check if Max's motorcycle was there. It's gone, and the Fiat isn't there either."

No one in the room made a sound as they tried to absorb the sobering truth. There weren't going to be easy answers. Elizabeth was missing.

His face grim and taut with tension, Ned Wakefield picked up the phone again. "I'm calling the police."

Max Dellon eased his motorcycle through the entrance gate and entered the hospital parking lot. Visiting hours long since over, there weren't many cars parked there. Max slipped his bike into an empty spot close to the hospital entrance. He took off his helmet and locked it on the side of the bike, then turned up the collar of his black jacket to ward off the wind. He headed toward the main building of the hospital, through the section of the parking lot marked Employees Only. Then he spotted a red Fiat convertible with the top up. Elizabeth's car.

"So she's working late," he said aloud. "The least she could have done was call me."

In anger Max kicked the left rear tire of the car. He'd been counting on Elizabeth to pull him through this test. She had no right to stand him up so thoughtlessly—and he planned to let her know how he felt.

And then he saw something lying on the ground. He moved toward it for a closer look and found that it was a scarf. Was it Elizabeth's scarf? he wondered. Looking up, he noticed that the door on the driver's side was partially open.

Max grew nervous. Something was wrong. A person just didn't get out of a car and forget to close the door. He peered inside the Fiat. "Oh, my God," he muttered softly, "something's happened to her!" Her sweater was on the seat. It was an unusually cool evening, and he knew she wouldn't have deliberately left it behind.

He pulled the car door open the rest of the way and climbed inside, looking for further signs of what had happened. On the floor, under the driver's seat, he discovered Elizabeth's purse. Maybe there'd be something there, a name, a phone number, or anything that might shed some light on her disappearance.

He settled down behind the steering wheel and dumped the contents of Elizabeth's bag onto the passenger seat. Using the dim car light for illumination, he pawed through her wallet, her makeup case, the little notebook she always carried around with her.

Finding no useful information in her pocketbook, he decided to try the glove compartment. Something was jammed in the lock, and he had trouble opening it. After fiddling with it awhile, he finally pried it loose. Like an overfilled suitcase, the tiny space had been stuffed with a variety of items ranging from half a pack of chewing gum to a broken nail file to a paperback book.

Max was so involved in his search that he didn't notice the flashing red lights of the police car as it entered the hospital parking lot. His hand was still in the glove compartment when an officer approached. "Just what do you think you're doing, kid?"

Max whipped around and squinted into the flashlight beam aimed at his face. He knew he wasn't doing anything wrong, but he doubted that anyone would believe him. It didn't take much to realize that sitting in someone else's car, going through someone else's belongings, looked incriminating.

He had no choice but to tell the truth. "Something happened to a friend of mine. This is her car. I was looking around to find some clues."

"Ah, a regular Sherlock Holmes, eh?" The policeman clearly didn't believe him. "Where's your trenchcoat and magnifying glass?"

"Honest, officer. I wasn't doing anything wrong. This is my friend's car."

"Sure," the officer said sarcastically, "and my name is Santa Claus."

Just then the other officer approached. "You all right, Sam—" He looked down at Max and nodded as he recognized the boy. "Hey, you're, uh, Dellon, right?" The gruff, middle-aged man had an all-knowing sneer on his face. "Looks like we got you red-handed this time."

Max gulped. He recognized the policeman too. It was the same one who'd questioned him outside the 7-11 several weeks earlier. Max had gone there one night after a particularly late session with the band. The policeman had pulled him over to his patrol car and accused him of "suspicious behavior." Max had been incensed— he was only trying to get himself a soda and a candy bar—and his surliness hadn't gone over well with the officer. He'd been let off with a warning, but he'd come close to being charged with harassing a police officer.

He wasn't going to make the same mistake twice. "No, sir," he said politely. "I was just explaining to the other policeman that this is my friend's car. She was supposed to meet me tonight, but she never showed up—"

"I get it. Some girl stood you up. So you decided to make off with her car."

"No!" Max shouted. "I'm telling you the truth. I think she's in trouble!"

The second officer grabbed Max's arm, yanked him out, and threw him against the side of the car. Max offered no resistance as the man slapped a pair of handcuffs on him. "You've got it wrong, kid. You're the one in trouble. The next time a friend of yours disappears, try calling the police," he said. "Your story doesn't wash, Dellon. You're under arrest."

Nine

Elizabeth opened her eyes groggily and once again faced the nightmare that refused to go away. She must have fallen asleep, she thought, but she didn't know for how long. In this new, dimly lit world she'd been placed in, it was impossible for her to tell whether it was day or night. She wished she hadn't decided to leave her watch on her bedroom dresser. Time had suddenly become so important to her.

Her muscles ached from having slept sitting up, and she longed to get up and stretch. But she could do nothing to relieve the pain. She was bound securely to the wooden chair, a chair that, for the time being at least, was her new home.

She was cold. She was hungry. And she was scared.

She had been so sure that Carl was going to kill her for trying to leave that she'd already pictured herself halfway to heaven. She knew she'd never forget that look in his eyes as he pulled her from the door—it had been a crazed mixture of fury, disappointment, and confusion. But he hadn't attacked her. Instead, he'd simply stood over her trembling body, staring at her. And then, to Elizabeth's astonishment, the big, clumsy man had burst into tears. He shook with great, heaving sobs, falling on the sofa next to Elizabeth. She hadn't known how to react. She'd never seen anything like that before. And she was terrified of what Carl might do in this state of hysteria. After a few minutes, she willed herself to look at him. "I'm still here," she'd told him in an effort to quiet him down. "I'm not going to leave."

Apparently it had worked, for a little while later Carl stood up and smiled, all traces of his earlier anguish gone. Yet his trust in Elizabeth had been shattered, and before he went to bed in the other room, he retied her to the wooden chair.

Now, in the early morning hours, Elizabeth could hear him snoring. She didn't understand how he could sleep so soundly after having kidnapped her, but then she didn't understand what had made him abduct her in the first place. Did he really expect her to love him just because he wanted her to? Did he really expect to keep her there forever?

Elizabeth didn't see how he could get away with it. With escape now out of the question, she turned her thoughts to rescue. She was surprised it hadn't occurred to her earlier, but then she had been so frightened that she couldn't think straight. Now she felt confident that rescue was inevitable. It was only a matter of time before the police would find her car and send out a search party. She couldn't remember whether or not Carl had left any fingerprints on it, but even if he hadn't, he'd be a prime suspect. If his oddball behavior had aroused her suspicions, it must have been noticed by others at the hospital as well. True, you couldn't arrest someone for being strange, but Carl was likely to call attention to himself anyway when he didn't go in to work on Sunday. Sunday! she thought, suddenly alarmed. What if he had Sunday off? But most of the employees were on rotating schedules, and chances were that Carl would have to work that day. And when he didn't show up, someone was bound to make the connection.

Elizabeth felt her spirits rise. All she needed was patience, and everything would work out fine. With a little luck she'd be home, sleeping in her own bed by Sunday evening.

A few minutes later Elizabeth heard sounds from the other room. Carl was up, and she got ready to put on the performance of her life. She wouldn't try to resist him or play games anymore. She'd be as nice to him as she could, to make sure he didn't get out of control. She felt confident that she could keep up the charade for the few hours it would take the police to find her.

Carl entered the room. He was wearing the same sweater and baggy pants he'd worn the evening before. It looked as if he'd slept in them. "Good morning," he said, smiling at her.

"Good morning," Elizabeth forced herself to answer, as if it were the most normal thing in the world to say to someone who'd tied you up the night before. "Did you sleep well?"

"Like a baby," he said. "Are you hungry?"

Elizabeth couldn't ignore the pangs in her stomach any longer. "Yes, I am," she admitted.

"Good. I've got a treat for you. I brought it in with me last night. Pancakes."

"Pancakes!"

Carl seemed proud of himself. "I overheard you telling Mrs. Willoughby how much you liked your mother's pancakes. I knew you'd be pleased." He walked across the room to the kitchen and took a box of frozen pancakes out of the refrigerator. They'd thawed somewhat, having spent the night on the bottom shelf instead of in the freezer compartment. It made no difference to Carl, though. He slapped the entire contents of the box into a pan on his hot plate.

As breakfast was cooking he returned his attention to Elizabeth, first helping her to the bathroom, then retying her to a chair at the kitchen table.

He went over to the stove, returning moments later with two pancakes. He set one down in front of Elizabeth. "Oh, I forgot to buy syrup," he said apologetically. "Do you mind eating them plain?"

"No," Elizabeth answered. "But how am I going to eat them if my hands are tied?"

"I'll feed you." Pulling the other chair next to her, Carl sat down and cut the pancakes into bite-size pieces. "I've seen you feed people in the hospital like this," Carl said, holding a forkful up to Elizabeth's mouth.

The dry pancakes looked like miniature Frisbees and tasted no better, but Elizabeth was too hungry to be discriminating. She was grateful Carl wasn't starving her. She finished everything he gave her, including the glass of milk he offered afterward, "to wash it all down."

After Carl put the dishes in the sink, he picked up a paper bag and placed it in front of

Elizabeth on the table. Almost shyly he said, "I found out you like to read. I hope you like these." He pulled three books out of the bag and laid them side by side in front of her.

Elizabeth looked them over. They were paperbacks, the kind that were readily available from the hospital gift shop. Carl hadn't chosen his selections carefully. One dealt with the strategy of investing, one was a book on raising farm animals, and the third was a collection of bedtime stories for children. She had no use for any of them but didn't want to hurt Carl's feelings. "Thank you very much," she told him. "I'm sure I'll enjoy these."

"I didn't know what to get. See, I can't read, so I took the first three I came to." Carl beamed as he disappeared into his bedroom.

He returned a few minutes later, and Elizabeth's jaw dropped when she saw what he was wearing: his orderly's uniform. "What have you got that on for?" she asked, almost afraid to hear his answer.

"I'm going to work now."

"You are? I thought you were going to call in sick." She tried to keep the panic out of her voice.

"No." The thought clearly hadn't entered his mind. "I don't have a phone."

"Oh." Elizabeth held back the tears. She knew that going to work was the smartest thing Carl could do. But did he? She had to get him to stay there with her. "Don't you want to spend the day with me?"

"Yes, Elizabeth. I want to spend every day with you. That's why I'm going to work now. I'm not stupid, you know. People are going to be looking for you today. The safest thing for me to do is to go about my business as usual."

"But what am I supposed to do?"

"I thought the books would keep you busy. Is there anything else I can get for you while I'm out?"

"A sweater, maybe? It's awfully chilly in here."

"I'll see what I can do. I don't want you to be cold. Let me get my blanket for you."

Before Elizabeth could protest, Carl came back with an old army blanket. He placed it gently on her shoulders. Then he loosened the ropes that bound her wrists—just enough to give her the minimum mobility she needed to turn the pages of her books. Then he quickly headed toward the door. "I'm running late," he said before slamming the door shut.

Once again Elizabeth was alone. She had no idea how long she spent trying to struggle out of the ropes, but as before, Carl had tied them securely. She finally stopped trying, giving in to a torrent of tears. Eventually, her sobs subsided. Then she lowered her right arm against the seat of her chair, and with the fingernail of her thumb she gashed out a notch. "Day one," she said grimly, wondering if there would ever be an end to this horror.

Ten

They were the four longest hours of Max's life.

The ride to the police station was the worst of it. Officer Michael Hadley, the one who'd recognized him from their earlier encounter, had tried, convicted, and sentenced him during the half-mile ride. "You'll like juvenile hall," the officer sneered, talking to Max's image in the rearview mirror. "Living with your own element, sharing a cell with a no-good thief just like you. 'Course you'll always have to keep on your toes, never knowing when one of your friends might pull a knife on you."

Max said nothing. He liked to pretend he was tough and strong, but right then he was really scared. He'd heard stories of what went on in the county juvenile detention center—and being threatened with a knife was the least of it. Guys who made it that far were mean and capable of doing anything to anyone. What those toughs would do to someone like him, a pushover by comparison, was something he didn't want to deal with at all. Yet he couldn't wipe the thoughts out of his mind. His only hope was that there was justice in the legal system and that someone would believe he had only been trying to do the right thing.

On top of his own fears, Max couldn't help worrying about Elizabeth. What *was* her car doing there, with the door partly open and her pocketbook still inside? The only thing that made sense was that someone had snatched her. But who? And why?

Of course the police wanted to know the answers to those questions, too, and for the next several hours they drilled Max mercilessly. Where had he been all evening? How well did he know Elizabeth Wakefield? Resolutely Max stuck to his story, repeating over and over again that it was his concern for her that had prompted him to go out and look for her. From the looks in the officers' eyes, it was clear that none of them believed him. But he had no defense other than the truth and never wavered for a moment.

In the end the police had no choice but to release him. They had no proof that he'd done anything other than go through a girl's belongings. He hadn't taken anything, and there was no evidence that he had broken into the car in the first place, not with the keys still in the ignition. But Max knew they'd be watching him closely, that until Elizabeth was found he'd remain a prime suspect.

He was never happier to see anyone than his parents, who were waiting for him in the lobby of the police station. He ran to his mother and hugged her with more intensity than he had since he was little. But when he looked up at the glaring, smoldering expression on his father's face, he was struck with the awful notion that, perhaps, the worst was yet to come.

None of the Wakefields slept much that night. When Steven came home from his date and learned what had happened, he had insisted on going out and searching for Elizabeth. Todd went with him, while Jessica and her parents remained in the living room, waiting for the phone to bring them word that Elizabeth had been found safe and sound.

The call didn't come, and when the boys returned, exhausted from combing the streets of Sweet Valley, they had no good news to report either. There were no signs of Elizabeth anywhere. She'd vanished without a trace.

Desperate for some plausible explanation, Todd

had just about managed to convince himself that Max Dellon was behind Elizabeth's disappearance. "How could the police have let him off so easily?" Todd stormed around the Wakefield living room. "He must know something he's not telling. I say we go over and confront him right now."

"His parents wouldn't let you talk to him earlier. What makes you think they'd let you now?" Steven asked. "Besides, I doubt that Max knows any more than you or I do. From what I know of him, he likes to talk tough, but on the inside he's a really decent guy. You ought to know that as well as I do."

"Maybe you're right, Steve," Todd conceded, "but I can't believe Liz would just . . . disappear. . . ." His voice cracked, and a single tear trickled down his cheek.

Steven laid a reassuring hand on Todd's shoulder. "I know how you feel," he said. "We'll go out again after sunup," he added. "As soon as there's light, we can search the parks and up through the hills." What he left unsaid, what he dared not say aloud, was that by then, they might be searching not for Elizabeth, but for her dead body.

Several hours later an exhausted Alice Wakefield rose from the easy chair, where she'd dozed off briefly, and headed for the kitchen for her Sunday-morning ritual. She knew she had to go on with life as usual if she was to keep her sanity during this shattering ordeal.

It seemed terribly unreal, she reflected as she put up a pot of coffee. Just the day before the whole family had been together in this very room, gathered around the kitchen table. Now Elizabeth was gone. And Mrs. Wakefield couldn't accept the awful speculation made by the police after they let Max Dellon go. They'd strongly hinted to her husband that perhaps Elizabeth wasn't missing. Perhaps she'd run away. The family had dismissed that notion. They knew Elizabeth would never run away from anything. Besides, Elizabeth had been so happy lately; what possible reason would she have to deliberately hurt her family this way?

Still, with the police entertaining this possibility, Mrs. Wakefield realized they might not put much effort into searching for her daughter. If that happened, it would be up to the family and friends to find Elizabeth.

After a while she called into the living room, "Breakfast's ready."

No one was in the mood to eat, but Mrs. Wakefield stressed the importance of trying. "You've got to eat, Steven," she coaxed her son. "For Liz's sake you've got to. You can't go searching for her on an empty stomach. You'll need your strength."

Mrs. Wakefield hadn't spoken to her son like

that in years, and her motherly chiding had its effect. "You're right, Mom," Steven said as he dug into the french toast she'd put before him. "Thanks."

Alice Wakefield also coaxed Todd, who had kept the long vigil with her family, to put some breakfast in his stomach.

But there was nothing she could do to make her daughter eat. Jessica stared at the plate in front of her. How could she think of food when her sister might be starving in some God-awful place?

And why? Because she, Jessica, had been too wrapped up in her own affairs to give a minute's thought to her twin. Someone else might have taken Elizabeth, yet she held herself responsible for her sister's disappearance. The litany of "what if's" she'd composed during the night replayed in her head. What if she'd paid attention to the hints her intuition had given her? What if she'd waited for Elizabeth to return? What if she'd followed through on her urge to call her sister at Max's before she'd left for the party? What if she hadn't lied to Todd? All that might not have prevented Elizabeth's disappearance, but it would have made everyone aware of it hours earlier. Valuable hours, time that might have enabled the authorities to catch up with the culprit.

And then there was Max. People often assumed the worst about him. He hung around Sweet Valley with some real bad-news types; and his metal-spiked wristbands and the scowling expression he wore around school didn't help. But Jessica agreed with Steven: Max's bark was worse than his bite. She couldn't imagine him doing anything to harm Elizabeth, especially when he was counting on her help in Mr. Collins's English class. Nevertheless, Jessica was more than a little angry at him. She knew, though, that she couldn't hold Max entirely responsible. If she'd reported her sister missing earlier, Max might never have gone to the car in the first place.

No matter how she looked at it, Jessica kept coming back to the same shameful realization—she had no one to blame but herself.

Eleven

What bothered Elizabeth most was the absence of light.

Not that it was completely dark in her ramshackle hideaway; Carl had left on the overhead light for her to read by, but the dim bulb cast an eerie glow in the room and formed shadows in the corners that served only to heighten her fear.

If only she could see the sun! But every window was boarded over. In the tiny cracks between the slats of wood, only wafer-thin streams of light shone through. And they weren't enough to make up for the claustrophobic feeling caused by being confined in that small room.

What could make someone do this to another human being? Elizabeth wondered as she struggled fruitlessly against the ropes that held her to the little wooden chair. Carl claimed to love her, yet he'd taken her away from everything and everyone in her life. He'd cloistered her in what was no better than a prison isolation cell. Her muscles ached from not moving; she was terrified; and above all, she was unbearably lonely. It occurred to Elizabeth that perhaps Carl felt this kind of loneliness all the time. Was that what had driven him to his senseless abduction? Whatever was behind his desperate, irrational behavior, Carl was running free, while Elizabeth was a captive.

She wondered what was going on outside the boarded-up hovel. Were the police looking for her? Did anyone have any suspicions about Carl?

Then thoughts she'd been trying to repress since the beginning of her ordeal began to push their way to her consciousness. Thoughts about her family and Todd. It pained her terribly to imagine what they were going through. She knew they were sick with worry. If only there were a way she could get a message to them to let them know she was still alive.

She couldn't count on Carl to help her out. This wasn't an ordinary kidnapping. There wasn't going to be a ransom note. He didn't want money. All he wanted was her—in his own twisted way.

And poor Jessica must be so worried about her! She figured her sister must have been the first one to realize she was gone. *She probably missed the Morrows' party on my account, waiting around the house for me to show up,* Elizabeth thought, heaving a deep sigh. She wondered where her twin was right then. More than anything, she wished she could be with her.

At that moment Jessica sat in her bedroom, staring blankly into space. At her mother's insistence she had changed out of the grubby clothes she'd thrown on the night before and was wearing an old pair of jeans and a cotton-knit sweater. She was a pale imitation of her usual self. Her vibrancy was gone, and in its place was an unusual mixture of helplessness and self-loathing.

With detached interest Jessica thought about the activity going on in the living room. Lots of people from the neighborhood and many of her friends were coming to the house to offer comforting words and support. But she felt they were wasting their time. Their gestures reminded Jessica of a hive full of bees—lots of frenetic movement that went nowhere. Every inch of Sweet Valley and the surrounding areas had been combed several times for any sign of Elizabeth. To no avail. Now there was nothing to do but wait and pray that some new clue would turn up.

Downstairs, the house was full. In the center

of things was Mr. Collins, who'd come over as soon as he had heard the news. Their next-door neighbors, the Beckwiths and the Kilgartens, were there too. Even her father's law partners had come to the house. Among Elizabeth's friends there was Enid, who'd wept in Jessica's arms on her arrival, and Elizabeth's co-workers on the Sweet Valley High newspaper, *The Oracle*, Olivia Davidson, Penny Ayala, and John Pfeifer. About a dozen other concerned kids from school were also there.

After sitting with the crowd for a short while, Jessica had fled up to her room. She couldn't bear to talk to anybody. That was why she was particularly annoyed by an insistent knock on her door. "Go away," she said angrily.

"Jessica, please let me in. I want to talk to you."

The voice was totally unexpected. Thinking she would send the boy off with a polite apology, Jessica rose to open the door.

There stood Nicholas, a paper shopping bag in one hand and her coat in the other, "I hope you don't mind. Your mom said it was OK to come up here. I wanted to let you know I'm so sorry about your sister," he said. "Regina is, too. It must be so awful for you."

Twenty hours earlier the idea of Nicholas in her bedroom would have been fodder for scads of fantasies, but now that he was there, Jessica found herself not caring. "They're forming search parties for her," she said in an uncharacteristically flat voice. "If you want to help, go ask Mr. Collins."

"I will. Later," he said. Then he held out the bag and coat for Jessica to take. "I brought your clothes. I thought you might want them."

"Thanks." Jessica took them and tossed them listlessly on her bed.

Nicholas looked at her. "Do you want to talk. You look like you can use a friend."

Jessica shrugged.

"Come on, Jess. This ordeal must be killing you, and I'll bet anything you're holding a lot inside." He took her hand. "Believe me, it'll make you feel better to get it out."

"You don't understand."

"Try me. It might help."

Nicholas's kind words and soft persuasion broke down Jessica's resistance. "OK," she said. "Let's go for a walk. I could use some fresh air."

They went outside and strolled slowly down the sun-streaked sidewalk. Neither of them said anything for a few moments. Finally Jessica broke the silence.

"Liz is a very special person."

"She must be," Nicholas said. "What's she like?"

"On the outside she looks exactly like me,

but inside she's everything I'm not." With rising hysteria Jessica spat out, "She never would have done to me what I did to her last night!"

"Hey, it's all right." Nicholas rubbed her back as Jessica was overcome by uncontrollable waves of tears.

"No, it's not all right!" Her wet eyes blazed as she spun around to face him. "It's my fault Liz is out there, probably being held hostage by some maniac. Or worse. If I'd shown just half the concern for her that she always does for me, she'd be here right now!"

"Whoa, Jess." Nicholas held her by the arms. "I'm not sure what's going on here, but I don't see how you could be responsible."

"But I am! I should have known Elizabeth was in danger last night! I should have known long before Todd had to drive it into me by pushing me into the pool. I should have, Nicholas, but I didn't. And it was my own fault."

"Why?" Nicholas looked puzzled.

"Because . . . because . . ." It was so hard for Jessica to get the words out. "Because I was too busy paying attention to you to think about Liz." She couldn't bear to see Nicholas's reaction, so she lowered her gaze, staring at the toes of her sneakers.

Nicholas took her face in his hands and gently tilted her head up toward his. "I don't believe that," he said.

"It's true," she answered, not caring now that he knew. "It was no accident that I was the first one at the party, and I was in such a hurry to get there—to meet you—that I didn't bother waiting for Liz to come home."

"I see," Nicholas said, a glint of amusement pushing through his worried expression for a split second. "But how does that make you responsible for her disappearance?"

"Don't you get it?" Jessica cried, the facts crystal clear and indisputable in her eyes. "I should have guessed something had happened when I got to the party last night. Liz was late, and she's the most reliable person I know when it comes to being someplace on time. I should have tried to look for her then—not hours later."

Nicholas pulled Jessica toward him, trying to soothe her. "I think you're being much too hard on yourself. Just look at what happened. Your sister probably disappeared a good hour before you even expected her home. You couldn't have done anything to prevent it."

"Tell that to Todd and my parents!" Jessica said bitterly.

"Do they blame you?" Nicholas asked.

"They don't have to. I can see it in the way they look at me."

"Don't you think you're being just the slightest bit unfair to them?" Nicholas asked gently. "I'm sure they don't blame you any more than I do. And for whatever it's worth, I know what you're going through."

"Nobody can understand," Jessica insisted.

"No?" Nicholas challenged. "I went through the same thing eight years ago, when I was ten and Regina was eight. My family had rented a summer house in Maine, an old log cabin on a cliff overlooking the ocean. Well, one afternoon my parents left me to watch Regina while they went boating with friends. Regina and I were in that stage where we hated each other, so I let her do what she wanted and didn't pay much attention to her. A couple of hours after my parents left, a fire broke out in the lofts where Regina and I slept. I panicked and ran out the door. Regina didn't come out after me, but I was too scared to go back in the house to look for her. The house burned down, and for hours afterward I was convinced I'd killed her. I felt that I didn't deserve to live either. I was sure my parents felt the same way, too; that is, until my dad realized what was going on inside me. He told me that no one expected me to be a hero at the expense of my own life, that I was only human. I don't know if I understood what he meant by that then, but I do now. You acted in a very human way, Jessica. You didn't do anything to hurt your sister, and I'm willing to bet that you're the last person in the world

111

she'd blame for this. The situation was absolutely beyond your control."

Jessica listened patiently to Nicholas's story. He was one of the kindest people she'd ever met. But it wasn't enough. "Thanks for trying, Nicholas, but I'm not in the mood for fairy tales."

"Fairy tales? That was one of the worst things I ever went through, Jess."

"But Regina didn't die."

"Thank goodness, no. While I wasn't looking, she'd sneaked out of the house and gone exploring in one of the caves in the area. She came back later that evening."

"She came back," Jessica repeated bitterly, the tears beginning to flow again. "But I may never see my sister again!" Despairingly, she threw herself against Nicholas's chest and poured out her agony.

Elizabeth's heart soared with hope as a car pulled up to the shack and let out several loud honks of its horn. Someone was coming for her!

Almost immediately, her spirits plummeted back down to the soles of her hospital-white shoes as she heard a key turn in the front-door lock. No one was breaking down the door to save her. It was just Carl, home from a day's work. Seeing him did nothing to relieve Elizabeth's unbearable pangs of loneliness. His presence served only to remind her that she was in the hands of a madman and that she'd better get used to being alone in the days and—could it be possible?—weeks ahead.

Carl had bought some burgers and fries at a fast-food restaurant, and he now placed the bags on the table in front of which Elizabeth had spent the whole long, horrible day. She found the aroma of the hot food nearly torturous and hoped Carl would unwrap it right away. "When are we eating?" she asked as pleasantly as she could. The poor excuse for pancakes he'd given her that morning had hardly made a dent in her appetite, and the hunger pains she'd been experiencing since late that morning suddenly accelerated in intensity.

"In a minute," Carl said, taking off his jacket. He flung it carelessly in the corner next to the sofa. "First, I have something for you." From a brown paper bag he took out a blue cardigan. "I hope you like it. I got blue because it matches your eyes."

"Thank you," Elizabeth said, a glimmer of hope fighting its way through her despair. He'd done exactly what she'd wanted him to do— he'd bought something that might arouse the suspicions of the gift-shop clerk. She knew it was a long shot at best, but it was the only chance she had. "It's really beautiful."

"I'm so glad you like it. I want to make you

happy." Carl removed the rope that was binding Elizabeth's arms to the chair and draped the sweater over her shoulders.

"I know you do," Elizabeth said. "I bet the woman at the gift shop was surprised to see you buying a lady's sweater."

"Oh, I didn't go to the gift shop. On my break I walked over to a store across the street from the hospital."

Elizabeth's spirits deflated again, but at least her arms were now free enough to grab the bags of food. "You don't mind if I start eating, do you? I'm very hungry."

"Go ahead," Carl said. "I'll join you in a minute."

She was so hungry, the hamburger tasted like the best food she'd ever eaten. Elizabeth wolfed down the whole thing in a couple of minutes.

As she started to sip the milkshake he'd brought, Elizabeth asked, "How was work today?"

"The same as always," he answered, "except for the cops."

Elizabeth slammed her cup down on the table. "Cops? What happened?"

"They were all over the place asking questions about you. They even talked to me. 'Course I told them I had no idea what happened to you."

"Of course," Elizabeth repeated, her spirits sagging even further.

Carl turned a sickening, savage smile on Elizabeth. "They don't suspect a thing. Last rumor. I heard around the hospital was that they think you're a runaway."

"No!" Elizabeth cried. "They can't."

"Calm down. There's nothing to worry about. You're safe here with me."

"Yeah, tied up like a wild animal. Caged like a criminal."

"No, no," Carl said. "I don't like having to do this. But you're like a beautiful bird to me. So beautiful and yet so willful. I had to put you in this cage so you wouldn't fly away from me. But it won't be this way forever. Soon you'll be free."

"You mean you're going to let me go home?"

"Oh, no," Carl said seriously, "something much better. I know a place far away from here, up in the mountains. A beautiful place for someone as beautiful as you, with lots of trees and open fields and a stream you can bathe in. You'll never want to leave."

"Are you going to tie me up there?" she asked.

"I won't have to. This place is way up on a high mountain far away from any roads or any people. If you tried to leave, you'd get lost.

Anyway, I intend never to let you out of my sight."

"But your job—"

"I'm leaving the hospital. I have some vacation time coming to me, and then I'm never going back. Maybe they'll put two and two together and realize I took you with me, but by then we'll be far far away and beyond anyone's reach."

Elizabeth watched in horror as Carl's eyes began to take on a dreamy, faraway look. She couldn't tell whether this place was for real or existed only in Carl's imagination. But terror coursed through her body. Right now she was still in Sweet Valley, or at least somewhere in the area. Once she left she knew Carl's prediction would be right, and the chances of her being found would be slim. "When are we going?" she asked, almost afraid to hear the answer.

"Tomorrow night."

Twelve

Her long blond hair was the first thing Todd saw when he approached the locker area at school the following morning. Pulled back in a rubber band, it looked so much like Elizabeth's that for a brief moment he thought his wish had been answered, that she'd come to school that morning as if nothing had happened.

But miracles like that didn't happen in real life, Todd realized as the girl turned around. It was Jessica, looking as if she hadn't slept in years. She hadn't bothered to fix her hair either, which accounted for the uncharacteristic ponytail. "I'm surprised to see you here," Todd said.

"I suppose I could say the same about you," she replied. "It was Mom and Dad's idea. They said I wouldn't be doing anybody any good moping around the house all day."

"Your parents are right," said Cara Walker, who'd just approached the pair. "I guess you still haven't heard anything."

Jessica shook her head. "Nothing—and now Dad says he suspects the police aren't going to try anymore. They think Liz ran away."

"That's ridiculous!" cried Todd. "She would never do that."

"Tell that to the cops!" Jessica said bitterly. "They said if she'd been kidnapped, there would have been a ransom note by now. We're hiring a private investigator."

"They've got to keep looking," said Todd, his voice wavering. "They've just *got* to find her. Or *we've* got to find her." He gave the locker next to him a ferocious kick.

"Maybe you should find Max Dellon instead," said Lila Fowler, who had joined the crowd beginning to surround Jessica and Todd. "I'll bet he knows a lot more than he's told anyone."

"How can you be so sure?" Todd asked.

"It's obvious, Todd," Lila declared. "The guy was caught red-handed in her car. You can't tell me he's not guilty."

"He didn't do anything, Lila," Jessica put in.

"If he's so innocent, how come his parents won't let him speak to anyone?" Lila challenged.

"If he's guilty, how come the police let him

go?" Todd countered in Max's defense, but there was a tiny note of uncertainty in his voice.

"Look, Max sneaked out of his house for several hours on Saturday night, right? The same time that Liz disappeared. The way I figure it, he snatched her as she was coming out of the hospital, took her away someplace, then came back later to get her car. It was just a stroke of luck on his part that he got away from the cops." Lila gave Todd a pointed stare. "I think you ought to have a little talk with him if you want to find your girlfriend."

"Lila, since when have you become the big expert on Max?" Jessica spat out. "Everyone in this school loves my sister. No one here would do anything to hurt her. Not Max or anyone else. It must have been some—some maniac." Her face crinkled up as she unleashed a flood of tears.

Todd took a step toward Jessica and gave her a hug. "Calm down, Jess. It's going to be OK." But he wasn't so sure. Lila had planted a fresh seed of doubt in his mind. What made Jessica and her brother, Steven, so sure Max didn't know anything? In any case, it couldn't hurt to talk to him. At the worst, they'd be no better off than they were now.

*　　*　　*

At that moment Max was on his way to school, sitting in the passenger's seat of his mother's sedan. Since his release by the police, he had become a virtual prisoner in his own house, under the constant surveillance of his parents. They'd made it clear that he'd betrayed their trust for the final time when he'd left the house without permission. His arrest had both embarrassed and hurt them, and while they were confident he had nothing to do with the Wakefield kidnapping, they'd grounded him indefinitely. The only place he was allowed to go was to school.

He would have considered it almost a pleasure to be going to school that day—if it hadn't been for Mr. Collins's test. He'd spent his entire Sunday holed up in the basement, trying to study *Othello*, and by nightfall he thought he'd finally gotten a grasp on what Shakespeare was saying. But he had little confidence in his ability to convey that to Mr. Collins. He figured he was going to be heading right down to the administration office after the exam to sign up for summer school.

Max was so preoccupied by thoughts of the big test that he wasn't prepared for the reception he got when he walked into his first class. Word about Elizabeth had spread quickly, along with the news of Max's arrest. The room appeared divided on his guilt, with about half of his classmates staring at him as if he were a creature beyond redemption and the other half looking at him with ill-concealed pity. Either way Max hated to be the focal point of attention. It was one thing to crave it while playing onstage with The Droids, but quite another when it came with the brand of criminal attached to it.

By the time he made it to Mr. Collins's last-period English class, Max wanted nothing more than to get the exam over with and return to the confinement of his own home. He'd never had a particularly good time at school, but that had been a day to end all days. Everywhere he'd gone, he'd had to confront the cold stares of people who'd already convicted him of kidnapping Elizabeth Wakefield. It seemed that overnight, he'd become Sweet Valley High's version of Jack the Ripper.

Shortly after Max took his seat, Mr. Collins entered the room. Elizabeth's disappearance had shaken him; she was one of his favorite students as well as one of the most selfless people he'd encountered in his teaching career. His concern was written all over his face that afternoon. There were dark circles under his normally bright, cheerful eyes. New worry lines made his handsome face look older and haggard. Without much enthusiasm he put his attaché case on his desk, took out the test papers, and laid them out in front of him.

Before he passed them out, he looked over at the fourth seat in the last row. "Max, can I see you?" he asked.

Mr. Collins's voice contained no hint of anger or reprimand, but the mere act of being singled out made Max cringe. All he could assume was that Mr. Collins wanted to add his name to the growing list of people who were out to get him.

But Max was prepared to tough it out. Determined not to show any emotion, he approached the desk with his head held high. "What can I do for you?" he asked.

Mr. Collins pulled Max into a corner. Keeping his voice low he said, "I'm surprised to see you here."

Max felt his thin veneer of calm start to crack. "Where did you think I'd be? Jail?"

Mr. Collins looked hurt. "That was uncalled for, Max. For what it's worth, I know you had nothing to do with Liz's kidnapping."

"Well, that makes one of you."

"You know I'm not the only one, Max. And I know you've been through a lot this weekend. I'm prepared to excuse you from the test today. You can make it up later this week."

"No way!" Max's cry could be heard by the rest of the class. "No one's going to call me a quitter, Mr. Collins. I want to take it now."

"Are you sure?" Skeptical, Mr. Collins raised an eyebrow.

"No special favors. I'm taking it now," Max repeated.

"OK. If you insist." Mr. Collins watched Max walk back to his seat.

As Mr. Collins was handing out the tests, Max wished he had a crane to pull out the large foot he'd just put in his mouth. What had he been thinking? Mr. Collins had given him the golden opportunity he'd prayed for, and what had he done? He'd turned it down, letting his pride get in the way. Max added it to his growing list of all-time stupid decisions.

It was too late to change his mind, so he figured he might as well see how he could do. As he took his first look at the test questions, a curious, and new, feeling arose. He actually cared about doing well. And with all the hours he'd spent going over the material, Max knew that some of it had seeped through. The only thing he had to do was prove it.

In the first section of the test he had to match the play's characters with quotations. Methodically he read the list of the ten quotations, and, much to his delight, was reasonably confident about eight of them. He had to guess at the two he didn't know, but even the fifty-fifty chance he'd been left with was much better than he was used to.

The true-or-false questions were a little tougher, but he realized he knew the play well enough to make educated guesses—again, much better than his usual process of circling the T's and F's at random.

By the time he got to the final multiple-choice questions, Max began to feel as if he were home free. *I really understand this stuff*, he said to himself with increasing amazement.

For the first time he could remember, he wasn't the last person in the class to finish the test. He wasn't the first, either, but when he lifted his pen after marking the final answer, he looked over at Mr. Collins and gave him a thumbs-up sign. He was confident he'd passed the test, and if his hunch was right, he might even have come close to getting an A. Max felt he had a right to be pleased with himself. He'd called on a reserve that he hadn't known existed, and he'd made it work for him. And he'd done it all by himself.

"Stop right there, Dellon," Todd yelled, as he came up behind him in the hallway. "I want to talk to you."

Max turned around, ready to pounce. But when he saw who it was, he controlled the anger that had been building all day. "Hey, Todd, I'm really sorry about what happened to Liz," he said sincerely. He leaned against the wall to make way for the passing traffic.

But Todd wasn't interested in Max's sympathy. "I might as well get right to the point," he said, moving closer to Max. "Liz's brother and sister seem to think you're innocent. And maybe I should just take their word for it. But you were in her car just after she disappeared. Somehow, I'd feel better if you explained yourself."

"Look, Todd, there's nothing to explain. I don't know what happened to Liz. I don't know if someone ran off with her or why." He shook his head ruefully. "But I sure wish I did, 'cause that girl got me in a lot of trouble."

That was all Todd needed to hear. He dropped his books and grabbed one of Max's shoulders, threatening to knock him down. "You've got some nerve blaming Liz for your troubles! I suppose she told you to go rummaging around in her car the other night?" The anger in Todd's voice rose with each word until his neck was taut with the rage he was trying to control.

Max lifted his arms to shake off Todd's hold on him. "Hey, bud, I was worried about her. Just like you were."

"Knock off the phony sob story and tell me the truth," Todd cried, grabbing Max by his shirt collar this time. He glared at the shorter boy. "You must have seen something. A suspicious-looking person. Anything. And you're going to tell me now."

Max could hear the panic in Todd's words. "I don't know anything," he answered.

"You're going to tell me even if I've got to shake it out of you."

"I don't know anything!" Max insisted.

"You're lying." Todd snorted in disbelief. He let go of Max's shirt and in one swift move pulled back his right arm and smashed his fist into Max's chin.

The unexpected blow stung. Max rubbed his sore chin with one hand while he raised the other to strike a retaliatory punch. But it never reached its mark. He was forced to pull back as someone suddenly moved between him and Todd.

It was Jessica. "Stop it, you two," she shouted, using all her strength to pry the two boys apart. "You have no reason to fight. You're both on the same side."

"Stay out of this, Jessica," Todd said, his glare still focused on Max. "This is none of your business."

"Yes, it is," she declared. "I can't stand by and watch you pick a fight with an innocent guy. This is so unlike you, Todd. Max doesn't know anything more about Liz than you do."

Max looked gratefully at Jessica.

"Liz wouldn't want to be the cause of a battle like this," she continued. "You know that's the truth, Todd."

Todd let his arm drop limply to his side. Jessica was right. Elizabeth couldn't bear to see people fight.

"Besides," added Jessica, "Max isn't the guilty party."

"How do you know?" Todd asked.

"Because it wouldn't make sense. Liz told me how much trouble Max was in with his English class—and she told me how happy Max was that she was helping him. Right, Max?"

"Yeah, Todd, listen to her. It's the first sensible thing anyone's said around here all day."

"So, Todd," Jessica summed up her argument, "why on earth would Max want to hurt the one person who was prepared to help him?"

Todd considered Jessica's words. Perhaps he was judging Max unfairly. After all, he'd only meant to talk to the other boy. But he'd gotten so carried away, he hadn't even given Max a chance to explain anything. And for once, Jessica was right—fighting was not his style. Obviously Elizabeth's absence had taken a huge toll on him.

"Todd, when I went out looking for her and found the car, I knew something bad had happened to her," Max said candidly. "I thought I could find something inside that might give me a clue. I know now that was a pretty dumb thing to do, and if I had to do it over again, I'd probably call the police first. But it's the truth. I swear it."

Todd took a deep breath. "OK, Max. I'm sorry. I guess I have no choice but to believe you." Shame colored Todd's cheeks a deep shade of red. It wouldn't do to take his fear and frustration out on anyone else. Fighting with Max was not going to bring Elizabeth back.

"Todd, Max." Jessica looked from one boy to the other. "If we're going to find my sister, we all have to work together. It might be our only chance." Jessica's tired expression was transformed by a look of determination. "We can't let this get between us. And we can't give up."

"Well you can count on me," Max said.

"Me, too, Jess," Todd told her quietly. "But what can we possibly do?"

"I don't know exactly. But I think we should start at the most logical place—right at the scene of the crime."

With a new sense of purpose, the trio rushed out of the building, using the side door to avoid Max's mother, who was waiting for him outside the front entrance. They ran to the Sweet Valley High parking lot as fast as they could, jumped into Todd's car, and headed for Fowler Memorial Hospital.

Thirteen

Elizabeth scratched a notch in the chair next to the one she'd made the day before. She'd entered the second day of her new life as prisoner of and companion to the saddest, most mixed-up person she'd ever encountered. If he were true to his word—and she couldn't be sure—today would be her last day tied to this chair. While she was heartened by the idea of being taken to a place where Carl would not feel compelled to tie her down, she dreaded the journey. The farther away from Sweet Valley they went, the greater the likelihood that she would never be found. The chance of her going home might become nonexistent.

Stop it! she told herself. Deep down she realized that she couldn't give up hope, that she couldn't surrender herself to Carl and his crazy idea of love. But it was getting harder and harder to keep her optimism.

These two days had seemed like two years, and she felt as if they had changed her tremendously. She'd had to deal with things she'd never dreamed she'd have to cope with, such as the restriction of all her movements and lack of all human contact other than with Carl.

Then there were the things so basic to her everyday life that she'd never thought about being deprived of them. Things like being able to scratch her back or lie down when she was tired or go to the bathroom at will. It had been two days since she'd had a shower or brushed her teeth. She hadn't been able to, and the thought of having Carl do it for her made her stomach churn with revulsion. It was out of the question. If she ever got out of here, the first thing she'd want to do would be to spend five hours in her bathtub.

She also longed for sound—not just the human kind but the everyday noises that indicated she was still a part of the world. While at night there were the occasional muffled sounds of a distant neighborhood, in the daytime all was quiet, as if the world had packed up and gone away. There were no house sounds, no rattling of heating pipes, ticking of clocks, or dripping faucets. On top of this, Elizabeth had to deal with long bouts of cold and hunger.

The rest of the world was starting to feel like a memory. It was almost as if everything that had happened to her before the kidnapping had happened to another person in another lifetime.

To combat this feeling, Elizabeth willed herself to call up one memory after another of her friends and family. She sensed that it was vitally important to keep remembering—that it might be the only way to keep a hold on herself. In particular, she filled her mind with recollections of Jessica and her, from their first day in nursery school together to their latest adventure with Jeremy Frank. They had gone through so much together that Elizabeth felt she might survive this ordeal by thinking about the times they'd had.

Letting herself get caught up in the memory, she chuckled as she remembered one incident in particular. It concerned a bright-yellow, V-neck sweater that Jessica had given her for her thirteenth birthday. Elizabeth had thought the sweater was much too bright, but Jessica soon began to borrow it. Before long it was clear to Elizabeth that Jessica had bought it with the intention of wearing it herself.

Elizabeth was hurt that Jessica hadn't thought of getting her something that she wanted, so she retaliated. By "accident" she shrank the sweater in the washing machine but put it back in the drawer as if nothing had happened. The next time Jessica asked to borrow the sweater, she was furious to see what had become of it. She got back at Elizabeth with the closest weapon at hand, a pillow, and whacked her over the head with it. Elizabeth fought back, and before they knew it, they were well into what had to have been the longest pillow fight on record. By the time they'd called a truce, both girls were tired and giggled out and couldn't remember why they'd been mad at each other in the first place.

As that memory faded, Elizabeth called up a new one, this time about Todd. And after that, yet another one. This kind of exercise in introspection had often helped her with her writing. But right then she cherished those recollections more than she ever could have imagined. Right then they were all she had.

Fourteen

Max stood still in the cavernous main lobby of Sweet Valley's only hospital. He, Jessica, and Todd had gone there on a rush of emotion and out of a sense of duty, but now that Max was alone, he was unsure what to do next.

They had decided to split up, each covering a different section of Fowler Memorial. They had agreed to question everyone they could find who had been on the Saturday shift the day of Elizabeth's disappearance: asking where they were, who they saw, and what had happened. The trio could only hope that somewhere in all those observations was a piece of information the police had missed, a clue that would lead to Elizabeth's whereabouts.

Max surveyed the busy scene around him:

nurses in crisp white uniforms and rubber-soled shoes; doctors with bulging medical kits; and visitors to the hospital flowing in and out of the revolving doors. Where should he start? Could any of these people tell him anything about Elizabeth Wakefield? Finally, taking a deep breath, he approached the woman sitting at the information desk near the entrance. She didn't have much to say to him. Neither did any of the other people he spoke to on that floor, most of whom had already talked to the police and were not interested in retelling what they knew to a mere high school student.

Feeling frustrated but still determined to do whatever he could, and, not coincidentally, clear his name, Max took the elevator to the third floor. A short walk from the elevator banks led him to a waiting room, where he sidestepped a group of anxious-looking people and went down another corridor toward the nurses' desk.

"Excuse me," Max said nervously to the nurse on duty. "I'm investigating the disappearance of Elizabeth Wakefield, and I'd like to ask you a few questions."

The middle-aged woman peered through her glasses at Max. "You're not with the police, are you?" Her tone registered a note of doubt.

"No, ma'am, I'm a friend of hers. I wonder if you could tell me if she worked on this floor last Saturday?"

"That poor girl," the nurse said sadly, "such a sweet young thing."

Max's expectations were raised. "So she was working here Saturday?"

"Yes, she was. At least I think it was Elizabeth. You know it might have been her twin sister. I could never tell those two apart."

"Thanks." Max looked up and down the corridor. One end of the hallway was empty except for a dark, stocky orderly pushing a laundry cart. Max decided to stop him and ask him if he knew anything.

At the same time Jessica was leaving a room on the other side of the corridor. From the defeated slump of her shoulders as she moved toward him, Max knew she hadn't uncovered any more than he had.

Suddenly a cry split the air. "Elizabeth! What are you doing here?" Max watched in stunned amazement as the orderly pushed his cart past him and sped toward Jessica, panic written all over his face.

The call of her sister's name made Jessica stop dead in her tracks. Was Elizabeth here? What was happening? The orderly was still rushing toward her, still calling her sister's name.

Then it became clear to her. *He thinks I'm Elizabeth.* He seemed almost possessed, his eyes bulging out of their sockets, his voice desperate as he cried out her twin's name. Jessica looked for a way to escape. She spun on her heels, hoping to find safety in the nearest room, but Carl was too fast for her. He pinned her against the wall with the laundry cart as she yelled for help.

"Elizabeth, I don't know how you escaped. But I've got you now." Pushing aside the laundry cart, he grabbed at Jessica.

"No, you don't." From behind, Max tripped the lumbering orderly, who fell to the floor. Max then used the weight of his own body to keep the larger man pinned down, immobilizing him with a wrestling hold he'd learned in PE class.

The orderly continued to ramble, "My Elizabeth, what are you doing? What happened? I don't understand."

"Call the police!" Max shouted to the nurse on duty. Then to Carl he said, "Do you want to be with Elizabeth again?"

"Yes."

"Then tell me where she is."

"She's right here," Carl cried.

"That's right. I'm still here," Jessica told him, adopting her sister's slightly more subdued manner of speaking. Slowly she approached Carl, who was lying helplessly under the weight of Max's body. The orderly obviously had no idea that Elizabeth had a twin. And Jessica planned to play on that for all it was worth.

"I want to know how you got away," Carl said.

Jessica looked at Max. "It's OK, you can get off him now."

"You sure?" Max whispered.

"I want to talk to my good friend here." Her expression indicated she wasn't fooling around.

Max reluctantly eased himself off the stocky orderly. Jessica's hunch had been right. Carl continued to lie there like a freshly felled tree.

Jessica wanted to jump up and yell for joy. This was the man who'd lead them to her sister! But in a tremendous effort of will, she put a lid on her exuberance. She had to keep up this charade until the police arrived to question this man further. They'd know exactly how to handle him.

"Are you mad at me?" Jessica asked, her voice contrite and full of apology.

"Sort of. You spoiled the plans. I don't understand how you escaped."

"Oh, that's not important." Jessica was improvising as she went along, trying to imagine the conditions under which this man was holding her sister captive. "I—um—I got lonely for my friends at the hospital."

"What about our plans? Our trip to the mountains?"

So he'd been planning to take Elizabeth away. Jessica's elation at her sister's imminent recovery was overshadowed by the bitter hatred welling inside her. This man wanted to take Elizabeth away from her. She quelled her rising fury. She knew she had to keep the orderly calm until he was securely handcuffed and in the charge of the authorities. "We can still do that. Right after your shift is over," Jessica answered him.

"Does that mean you're coming back with me?"

"Of course," Jessica said simply.

It wasn't until two policemen slapped handcuffs on his wrists and read him his rights that Carl realized what was really happening. As he was being led away, he called out to the tall blond now weeping with relief on Max's shoulder. "Elizabeth, why are you doing this to me? All I wanted to do was make you happy."

Jessica looked up at the man with ill-concealed hatred, glad she could shed her assumed identity. "I'm not Elizabeth. I'm her sister, Jessica. You weren't making her happy. You were keeping her from everyone she loves. But not anymore. Not anymore, thank goodness."

A few minutes after that, Jessica and Max found Todd talking to a young intern on the third floor. Jessica ran up behind Todd and grabbed him around the waist.

"Liz is alive!" she yelled. "She's going to be rescued!"

Todd whirled around, joy spreading across his handsome face.

"Yeah, Wilkins. Where were you? You missed all the excitement." Max grinned from ear to ear.

Then he and Jessica told the whole story, punctuating their narrative with smiles of happiness.

When they were finished, the three friends threw their arms around one another and quickly headed out of Fowler Memorial, looking to all the world as if they had just been handed a key to paradise.

An hour or so later, Jessica rode along with two policemen down a hill and past several blocks of run-down housing. Apparently, as soon as Carl realized his game was up, he confessed everything and told the police where they could find Elizabeth. They then saw the house, just as Carl had described it—a boarded-up dwelling at the end of St. James Avenue, isolated by vacant lots. The house looked empty, lifeless. Jessica couldn't believe her sister had spent the last two days there. She couldn't imagine anyone being able to survive such isolation.

Elizabeth heard a commotion outside. A police siren was getting louder and louder until finally it came to a stop so close that she was almost afraid to believe they might be coming for her.

Everything else happened quickly. A loud pounding on the door was followed by the arrival of the first friendly face she'd seen in almost forty-eight hours. "Are you all right?" the police officer asked.

"Now I am," Elizabeth responded joyously as the officer began to untie her.

"You're free, Liz!" Jessica cried happily, rushing into her sister's arms.

"Jess! I thought I'd never see you again."

"Oh, I bet deep down you knew I'd come to the rescue." She said it offhandedly, as if fending off a deranged man twice her size were something she did every day.

Elizabeth couldn't believe what had happened. "How did you trick him?"

"An old twin's secret," Jessica answered. "That ogre thought I was you!"

"I may live to regret these words someday," Elizabeth said, "but I'm so lucky to have you as my twin."

"I know."

The two sisters held each other close for the longest time, never before truly realizing how much they meant to each other. "I love you, Jessica," Elizabeth cried.

"Me, too," Jessica said. Her voice grew hoarse, and she sniffled a little.

"Hey, what's the matter?" Elizabeth asked, pulling back to look at her sister. "Don't cry. It's over. Everything's going to be fine, now."

"Who me? Cry over you? Impossible!" said Jessica. And then, once more, they hugged each other wildly.

Fifteen

"What's the first thing I want?" Elizabeth repeated the question her mother asked her after her happy reunion at home with the rest of her family, Todd, and Max. "First, I want to take a bubble bath. Then I'd like something to eat. Then I want to sit down with Jessica and plan the best party this town has seen."

Jessica, who always loved a good party, started making calls immediately. Later, Elizabeth joined her to plan the decorations and refreshments.

"I don't know how you were able to take it," Jessica remarked as she sat cross-legged on Elizabeth's rug. "I couldn't have stood it."

Elizabeth didn't answer at first. It was true that her sister thrived on happiness and good times and seemed to go to pieces when the music stopped, but Jessica had shown remarkable strength during this ordeal. It was her determination that had led to Elizabeth's return. Jessica was the heroine.

And she couldn't have done it, Elizabeth concluded, without some inner reserve to call on. "I think you would have managed," Elizabeth said.

"But to have had to wear that yucky candy striper's uniform all that time." Jessica pinched her nose with her fingers.

"Don't worry, I've already burned it." Elizabeth laughed.

"Liz, while we're speaking of clothes . . . I don't have anything decent in my closet to wear to this party."

"Jess," Elizabeth said with amusement, "the party's four days away."

Jessica looked at her sister incredulously. "Liz, it's never too soon for the hostess to plan her outfit."

"What about that?" Elizabeth pointed to the red velour skirt and white blouse that were still on her bed, where Jessica had put them the evening of Regina's party.

"No, thanks, they're not my style," Jessica hedged.

Elizabeth giggled. "I guess not. I'd forgotten all about that skirt, but someone dug it out of my closet. It was on my bed when I came home. Know anything about it?"

"No," Jessica fibbed. How could she tell her twin that she'd been casually choosing clothes for her to wear to the party, while Elizabeth had been lying bound and gagged in Carl's van? "Never saw it before. Uh—got anything else I could wear?"

"Well," Elizabeth said, smiling slyly, "there's always my yellow sweater."

"What yellow—?" Then Jessica remembered, and without hesitating a moment, she picked up a pillow from Elizabeth's bed and started the second longest pillow fight of their lives. . . .

On Friday night Elizabeth finished getting dressed and found Todd waiting for her in the den. They stared at each other silently, still filled with thanks that Elizabeth was back where she belonged. Then, predictably, like a bee to honey, they joined together, arms entwined, seemingly content to stay like that for the rest of the evening.

Elizabeth's mother passed by the door of the den on her way to the kitchen and glanced at the couple with concern. It wasn't that she was bothered by the caress itself—it was the intensity behind it that made her a bit nervous. Elizabeth and Todd had been dating steadily for quite some time now, and she was afraid their relationship might be heading toward something more serious. Mrs. Wakefield was fond of Todd, but both she and her husband feared that Elizabeth might be tying herself down too early. In that sense they wished she were a bit more like Jessica, who changed boyfriends with alarming regularity. But the few times she'd tried to broach the subject to Elizabeth, her daughter had cut her off with a brief, "Don't worry, Mom. I know what I'm doing."

That was exactly how Elizabeth felt, too, as she finally broke off her kiss with Todd. "You don't know how much I missed that," she whispered. Giggling, she added, "Then again, maybe you do."

"You're so beautiful, Liz." Todd's eyes were sparkling with happiness.

"In this?" Elizabeth pointed to her simple sweat-shirt dress.

"You know I'm not talking about your dress. You could be wearing a barrel, and I'd still think you were gorgeous."

"Well, I didn't look so great when you saw me a few days ago."

Todd's face clouded over. "Liz, it must have been so awful."

"But it's over," Elizabeth said emphatically. "Right now I just want to celebrate being here."

"Ready for an encore?"

145

"I thought you'd never ask."

Their kiss was interrupted by Jessica. "Excuse me, lovebirds, but our guests are starting to arrive." Following her into the room were Enid and her boyfriend, George Warren.

"Enid!" Elizabeth pulled away from Todd and rushed over to her friend. They hugged warmly.

The two girls had had a noisy reunion at school earlier in the week, but George, who attended nearby Sweet Valley College, was seeing Elizabeth for the first time since the kidnapping.

"You look wonderful," he told her as he kissed her on the cheek. "It's great to have you back."

The doorbell rang again. "I'll get it!" Jessica volunteered, rushing to answer it with the speed of a jet plane.

"Why the rush?" Enid wondered.

Elizabeth winked. "Jessica invited someone special over." Over the last few days, her sister had made no secret of her interest in Nicholas Morrow. Now that Elizabeth was safe and sound, Jessica was again turning her attention back to more pleasurable matters.

"I have a pretty good idea who it is," Todd offered, picturing Jessica in her black-and-white bikini, flirting madly with Nicholas at the side of his pool.

But it wasn't Nicholas at the door. It was Max Dellon, followed by the rest of The Droids. Now

146

that he had passed his English exam with flying colors, his parents had allowed him to play with the band again. And much to Jessica and Elizabeth's delight, The Droids had agreed to perform for their party.

As Max was setting up some of the band's equipment, Todd wandered into the living room and headed over in his direction.

"How's the star guitar player?" he asked warmly.

"Hey, if it isn't the guy with the mean right hook," Max tossed back, but he grinned to show there were no hard feelings.

Todd returned the grin. "You know, Max, that punch really made my hand sore."

"Well, now you've got Liz back to nurse you to health. And speaking of the luscious lady . . ."

Elizabeth ran over, bursting with news. "Guess what, everyone! I just got a phone call from Jeremy Frank. He wants me to come on his show and talk about what I went through."

"Are you up to it?" Todd asked.

"I think so," Elizabeth said. "Looking around here and seeing all my friends and the love they have for me—it really means a lot. Knowing you're behind me, I feel I can talk about that awful nightmare. . . ." She paused, then giggled impishly. "Besides, I can't turn down a chance to be on television."

"When are you going to be on?" Max asked.

"We're taping tomorrow," Elizabeth said. "And they want to air it within a few days. Jeremy said he wanted to have me on while I was still newsworthy." She turned to Jessica, who was standing nearby with Cara Walker and Lila Fowler. "Isn't that great, Jess! Just think, you and I will have been on the same TV show!"

"Yeah, great," Jessica said, trying to be enthusiastic for her sister's sake. But she hated being upstaged, even by Elizabeth. The program she'd taped with Jeremy Frank wouldn't be on for several weeks, and the event would no longer be a novelty now that her twin would be on the show first. At the same time, though, she really didn't want to put a damper on Elizabeth's good spirits, not so soon after the terrible events of the past week. "Excuse me, gang," she said, heading toward the kitchen to regain her composure. "I'll be back in a second with sodas."

As Jessica was busy playing hostess, the doorbell rang again. This time Elizabeth answered it. Her face was aglow with happiness as she opened the door.

On the opposite side of the threshold stood someone she didn't know. A boy—with the kind of handsomely chiseled features that looked as if they belonged on a magazine cover. "Jessica?" he asked, confusion apparent in his voice.

"Oh, no," she said with a friendly smile. "I'm Elizabeth. But don't feel bad—people mix us up all the time. And you're—?"

"Nicholas. Nicholas Morrow." He stated his name slowly, almost automatically, as he found himself concentrating all his attention on the girl standing before him.

"Well, come on in, Nicholas." Elizabeth waved him inside. "I'm glad to finally meet you."

"No, the pleasure is mine," Nicholas said, still staring at Elizabeth. "And let me apologize for confusing you with your sister. I'll never make that mistake again."

"I'll go tell Jessica you're here."

"No, that's OK. No hurry," Nicholas said. "I want a chance to tell you how glad I am that you're home. I was worried about you."

"But you don't even know me."

"That's not exactly true. Jessica has told me a lot about you. She made you sound like someone worth knowing—and I can see now that she's right."

There was no way Elizabeth could mistake the look she saw in his eyes, a look that said, "You're the one I want." It made her feel awkward and uncomfortable. She had a strong suspicion that Nicholas hadn't reacted this way with Jessica. And she dreaded what would happen when Jessica found out.

Will Elizabeth leave Todd for Nicholas? Find out in Sweet Valley High #14, **DECEPTIONS.**

	25033	**DOUBLE LOVE #1**	$2.50
☐	25033	**DOUBLE LOVE #1**	$2.50
☐	25044	**SECRETS #2**	$2.50
☐	25034	**PLAYING WITH FIRE #3**	$2.50
☐	25143	**POWER PLAY #4**	$2.50
☐	25043	**ALL NIGHT LONG #5**	$2.50
☐	25105	**DANGEROUS LOVE #6**	$2.50
☐	25106	**DEAR SISTER #7**	$2.50
☐	25092	**HEARTBREAKER #8**	$2.50
☐	25026	**RACING HEARTS #9**	$2.50
☐	25016	**WRONG KIND OF GIRL #10**	$2.50
☐	25046	**TOO GOOD TO BE TRUE #11**	$2.50
☐	25035	**WHEN LOVE DIES #12**	$2.50
☐	24524	**KIDNAPPED #13**	$2.50
☐	24531	**DECEPTIONS #14**	$2.50
☐	24582	**PROMISES #15**	$2.50
☐	24672	**RAGS TO RICHES #16**	$2.50
☐	24723	**LOVE LETTERS #17**	$2.50
☐	24825	**HEAD OVER HEELS #18**	$2.50
☐	24893	**SHOWDOWN #19**	$2.50
☐	24947	**CRASH LANDING! #20**	$2.50

Prices and availability subject to change without notice.

Buy them at your local bookstore or use this convenient coupon for ordering:

SWEET DREAMS are fresh, fun and exciting.—alive with the flavor of the contemporary teen scene—the joy and doubt of *first love*. If you've missed any SWEET DREAMS titles, from #1 to #100, then you're missing out on *your* kind of stories, written about people like *you!*

☐ 24460	**P.S. I LOVE YOU #1** Barbara P. Conklin		$2.25
☐ 24332	**THE POPULARITY PLAN #2** Rosemary Vernon		$2.25
☐ 24318	**LAURIE'S SONG #3** Debra Brand		$2.25
☐ 26613	**LITTLE SISTER #5** Yvonne Green		$2.50
☐ 24323	**COVER GIRL #9** Yvonne Green		$2.25
☐ 24324	**LOVE MATCH #10** Janet Quin-Harkin		$2.25
☐ 24832	**NIGHT OF THE PROM #12** Debra Spector		$2.25
☐ 24291	**TEN-BOY SUMMER #18** Janet Quin-Harkin		$2.25
☐ 26614	**THE POPULARITY SUMMER #20** Rosemary Vernon		$2.50
☐ 24338	**SUMMER DREAMS #36** Barbara Conklin		$2.25
☐ 24838	**THE TRUTH ABOUT ME AND BOBBY V. #41** Janetta Johns		$2.25
☐ 24688	**SECRET ADMIRER #81** Debra Spector		$2.25
☐ 24383	**HEY, GOOD LOOKING #82** Jane Polcovar		$2.25
☐ 24823	**LOVE BY THE BOOK #83** Anne Park		$2.25
☐ 24718	**THE LAST WORD #84** Susan Blake		$2.25
☐ 24890	**THE BOY SHE LEFT BEHIND #85** Suzanne Rand		$2.25
☐ 24945	**QUESTIONS OF LOVE #86** Rosemary Vernon		$2.25
☐ 24824	**PROGRAMMED FOR LOVE #87** Marion Crane		$2.25
☐ 24891	**WRONG KIND OF BOY #88** Shannon Blair		$2.25
☐ 24946	**101 WAYS TO MEET MR. RIGHT #89** Janet Quin-Harkin		$2.25
☐ 24992	**TWO'S A CROWD #90** Diana Gregory		$2.25
☐ 25070	**THE LOVE HUNT #91** Yvonne Green		$2.25

☐	25131	KISS & TELL #92 Janet Quin-Harkin	$2.25
☐	25071	THE GREAT BOY CHASE #93 Janet Quin-Harkin	$2.25
☐	25132	SECOND CHANCES #94 Nany Levinso	$2.25
☐	25178	NO STRINGS ATTACHED #95 Eileen Hehl	$2.25
☐	25179	FIRST, LAST, AND ALWAYS #96 Barbara Conklin	$2.25
☐	25244	DANCING IN THE DARK #97 Carolyn Ross	$2.25
☐	25245	LOVE IS IN THE AIR #98 Diana Gregory	$2.25
☐	25297	ONE BOY TOO MANY #99 Marian Caudell	$2.25
☐	25298	FOLLOW THAT BOY #100 Debra Spector	$2.25
☐	25366	WRONG FOR EACH OTHER #101 Debra Spector	$2.25
☐	25367	HEARTS DON'T LIE #102 Terri Fields	$2.25
☐	25429	CROSS MY HEART #103 Diana Gregory	$2.25
☐	25428	PLAYING FOR KEEPS #104 Janice Stevens	$2.25
☐	25469	THE PERFECT BOY #105 Elizabeth Reynolds	$2.25
☐	25470	MISSION: LOVE #106 Kathryn Maris	$2.25
☐	25535	IF YOU LOVE ME #107 Barbara Steiner	$2.25
☐	25536	ONE OF THE BOYS #108 Jill Jarnow	$2.25
☐	25643	NO MORE BOYS #109 White	$2.25
☐	25642	PLAYING GAMES #110 Eileen Hehl	$2.25
☐	25726	STOLEN KISSES #111 Elizabeth Reynolds	$2.50
☐	25727	LISTEN TO YOUR HEART #112 Marian Caudell	$2.50
☐	25814	PRIVATE EYES #113 Julia Winfield	$2.50
☐	25815	JUST THE WAY YOU ARE #114 Janice Boies	$2.50

Prices and availability subject to change without notice.

Bantam Books, Inc., Dept. SD, 414 East Golf Road, Des Plaines, Ill. 60016

Please send me the books I have checked above. I am enclosing $_____
(please add $1.50 to cover postage and handling). Send check or money order
—no cash or C.O.D.'s please.

Mr/Ms _____

Address_____

City_____State/Zip_____

Please allow four to six weeks for delivery. This offer expires 6/87.

Bantam Offers Zindel

Pulitzer Prize Winner
Paul Zindel

- ☐ 26425 Confessions of a Teenage Baboon $2.75
- ☐ 24741 The Effect of Gamma Rays on $2.95
              Man-in-the-Moon Marigolds
- ☐ 26486 The Girl Who Wanted a Boy $2.75
- ☐ 24394 I Never Loved Your Mind $2.50
- ☐ 24396 My Darling, My Hamburger $2.50
- ☐ 23975 Pardon Me, You're Stepping On $2.50
              My Eyeball
- ☐ 25397 The Pigman $2.75
- ☐ 26599 Pigman's Legacy $2.95
- ☐ 22694 A Star For the Latecomer $2.25
- ☐ 26601 To Take a Dare $2.95
- ☐ 26424 The Undertaker's Gone Bananas $2.75

- ☐ **25775 Harry & Hortense at Hormone High**   **$2.95**

Is Jason crazy, or is he the most exciting and dynamic person ever to hit Hormone High? Harry and Hortense decide to find out by helping Jason convey to the world his message of hope and prophecies of doom.

BANTAM
SHOP·AT·HOME
C·A·T·A·L·O·G

Special Offer
Buy a Bantam Book
for only 50¢.

Now you can have Bantam's catalog filled with hundreds of titles plus take advantage of our unique and exciting bonus book offer. A special offer which gives you the opportunity to purchase a Bantam book for only 50¢. Here's how!

By ordering any five books at the regular price per order, you can also choose any other single book listed (up to a $4.95 value) for just 50¢. Some restrictions do apply, but for further details why not send for Bantam's catalog of titles today!

Just send us your name and address and we will send you a catalog!